THE HUNTRESS OF CAERLIN

CHRIS TURNER

CONTENTS

1 : Isks of Doom   5

2 : The Magic Arrow   47

3 : The Last Hunt   85

CHRIS TURNER

1: Isks of doom

A gentle breeze rustled the treetops and Risgan the Relic Hunter paused to take a breath. He called ahead to his four companions to wait up. He clutched the handle to his enchanted wagon, a kind of barrow that carried the caged witch, Afrid. Her eyes glowered in distaste, rich with an unpleasant hue behind those dark withes of thorn. A godsend that her magic had been stripped by the piece of nephrite he kept stashed away in his pouch. But was the effect permanent? Her three foot height did not diminish her menace, despite confinement in that square cage of tough thorn.

"Seems Afrid's in a rotten mood this morning," mused Kahel the archer, lumbering forth, scratching an itch on his sweaty brow.

"Bully for her," said Risgan.

"Aye," mumbled Jurna the journeyman in a dark voice. His bushy brows dipped in a scowl. It seemed his memories of old wounds inflicted back at Thornkeep were still quite fresh.

Moeze the magician looked back at the trees from where they had come. "Thornkeep, bah! Perhaps, I shall learn useful spells from this hag before she gets her just desserts."

"Better luck talking to the devil," grumbled the archer, counting his precious arrows. Too few of them for the dangers that lurked ahead. He shook out his shaggy mop of red hair.

Afrid hissed between the thorn bars and rattled her cage with an unwholesome fervor. The witch's baby face and youthful skin seemed uncanny for one so utterly wicked and cruel. Her snake-like hiss had Risgan recoiling.

"Relax," Moeze chided. He flicked his fingers in the gesture of a spell...a bright green spot grew on the witch's brow. "Aiee!" she squealed in anguish. She clammed up after that.

Kahel laughed.

Risgan only stared at Afrid with dislike. He recalled how the witch had turned on the philosopher Delpit and transformed him into a mindless slave. Left him some shell of a man. Effectively killing him.

Risgan sighed. *And what of his own fate?* Pursued by Pantius's bounty hunters across the lands, he was little more than an outlaw. They had chased him practically to Afrid's doorstep. He and the others were lucky to have escaped Thornkeep, abode of the dark sorceress, and then only by the skin of their teeth. Aside from the fabulous gem in his pouch, he had only the black boots, leather breeches and jerkin on his back.

He studied each of his four new companions with fresh wonder. Kahel, Jurna, Moeze and Hape. Strange how fate had brought the five together. Bonded after their narrow escape from the witch's lair, they each guarded an inner fire for survival. Jurna, a journeyman, tracker, dark-haired and shaggy; young Moeze, a questionable magician, tall and spare, whose magic had not helped them much on their journey; Kahel, a grim-faced archer with a thick red beard, who was swift and strong; then Hape the Homeless, a thin-boned drifter, something of a vagrant whose meek temperament was offset by his knowledge of the wild lands.

Risgan turned his attention back to the witch. The powers of the nephrite stone had reversed her aging process, given her the face of a baby and the body of a four-year-old. He patted the sealed pouch at his side that housed the spell-laden nephrite. He too had handled the gem briefly and felt its taint. Mercifully, he hadn't been affected as much, though he felt his skin softer than usual and an uncanny spryness in his step.

Hunger had struck early that day. The wayfarers hunted quail and hare in the broadwood and scattered glades. Larger game if they could find it. A chill mist rose from the hollows and vales, leaving the lands naked. Before long they had a fire crackling in a sheltered lee by a small wooded hill. But they had scored only two small hares to glut the hungers of five ragged men. Few words were traded among the fugitives. It was time to move on, find more game and seek shelter before evening.

A glade of wild huckle-flowers loomed ahead. A lone dead elm stood tall in the center. At the fringe of the clearing, twitch trees soared on high, green as firs, willowy as willows, soft as deadmusk, a screen for stags and elk to hide behind and creatures much more dangerous.

The air was fresh and the spring birds chattered in numbers in the high boughs, adding a pleasant ambiance to the dwindling dawn.

Risgan knew better. These woods were as perilous as any in the four lands. He hoped to escape them before long.

Better hope for the devil! Though Jurna's tracking skills had, up till now, proven infallible, they found themselves utterly lost, heading in a northerly direction at best. Their bellies growled with greater hunger. Moeze yawned. He tugged at the hem of his wide sleeves. He fidgeted in his loose robe, grown rank and soiled from confinement in Afrid's keep for days on end. Brows furrowed, he murmured anxious words, as if playing over some mispronounced spell in his mind. Hape doddered listlessly at his side, wrapped in his brown, tattered monk's robe, mumbling phrases of encouragement to himself in no less cryptic manner. The tall twitchwood trees bore witness to the company's passing, heedless as the wind, silent as ghosts.

Hape sighed. "We'd best drop lines into the creek and wait an hour for some trout."

"Quiet," muttered Kahel. He turned to Risgan. "What do you want today, falcon or hawk?" His face showed a facetious grin.

"Neither. I prefer wild boar. The meat has a succulent flavor, gamy but tasty. Roasted, of course."

Kahel chuckled. "You'd not like to be surprised by one of those violent beasts."

"Not as bad as isks—"

His words were cut off as a flutter of motion caught Risgan's eye—a shrub rustling at the edge of the glade where the twitch trees thinned. He pulled his comrades back into the brush.

A slender figure poised in a bent-kneed crouch. A hunting bow was in her hand. Drawing an arrow from her quiver, she steadied her aim upon what looked like a majestic stag grazing a bowshot away. A smaller shape, a young foal with black and white pelt, ambled out of the bushes. It lifted its head then came trotting forward to brush its parent's muzzle, as trusting as ever. Risgan's eyes widened. Not a stag, but a full grown unicorn. The huntress lowered her bow.

"Wait." Risgan held Jurna firmly back.

Awestruck, the maiden advanced, only to pause a dozen feet before the mother and her foal. The mother unicorn nudged her young one forth; it sidled closer to greet the newcomer. The huntress dropped to a knee, then began to pet its black mane. She cooed with delight as it snuggled closer.

The mare's hide shimmered a deep purple hue; her proud white horn arched high. While the huntswoman patted the youngling's mane, the mother wandered over, as if intuiting no great threat.

The woman wore brown breeches and leather jerkin that blended well into the surroundings. A cascade of brown curly hair trailed down her back.

"That lass looks as if she knows the land," whispered Jurna. "Let's go question her. We're lost, let's admit it."

"And you the master tracker," jeered Kahel.

"Be careful not to scare her," Risgan warned. "The woman looks a bit skittish." Though he noted she moved with a grace and a defiant upward tilt of chin.

"No more skittish than the unicorn," Jurna observed.

"Be careful not to spook the unicorn. I've never seen one up so close before, let alone a foal."

"Maybe she possesses magic?" suggested Hape.

Moeze huffed out a laugh. "I detect no magic."

The maiden, wild and beautiful as the forest, continued to charm the young animal. The mother moved closer but halted at Risgan's approach. The mare lifted her head, cocked it on a suspicious angle then thumped her hooves. The young woman's head turned in surprise. She snatched at her bow, gazed at the newcomers, no more than a shaggy band of forest rovers come out of nowhere. Her hand drew the bowstring taut. "Halt! Stay where you are!"

A flutter of wings echoed from above. Risgan's head rose. A dark shape loomed out of the cloudless sky. His jaw tightened.

"Isks. I hate isks," Kahel growled as he nocked an arrow.

The gigantic bird dove toward the maiden and gave a raucous croak. The air seemed to bend with the advance of the black-feathered predator, a monstrous raven-like creature, several times larger than a man, with a huge, tapered beak.

"I can manage this." Moeze said as he lifted his silver disc. A crafty glint shone in his greenish eyes, as if seeing his chance.

"*Nastanderlist. Exeunt!*"

Risgan reached out a hand. "Don't—"

A gleam of magical radiance sputtered out of Moeze's crystal disc. It smote the tree next to the huntress, surprising the winged predator. A boom of distant thunder came from afar; a pale silver light seemed to touch the top of the trees near the bracken where she and the unicorns hunched undercover. The nearby twitchwood tree split and toppled, nearly crushing them all, leaving the isk unscathed.

"You idiot!" Kahel cried, cuffing Moeze on the head.

"Ow! What was that for?"

"Focus on the isk!" said Jurna.

The huntress took aim and fired; her arrow grazed the isk's belly, prompting a screech. Kahel's first arrow caught the beast sideways on the wing, but it deflected off, falling harmlessly to the ground.

She fired again; this time the arrow plunged deep in the flesh above a talon and stuck there, stirring the beast to frenzy. In a flurry of outstretched wings, it flapped down to gut her. She ducked the murderous sweep of its claws while the mother unicorn reared, striking the beast with its sharp hooves in the beak.

The bird croaked and reached out to gore the mother in the vulnerable flank. She gave a shrill whinny and arched aside, hooves flailing. A trail of blood dripped from her sleek flank.

A second grayer shape, an older isk, veered down with equal menace.

Then another. The bird landed aside the young woman who leapt sideways and drew her blade, slashing out with fierce desperation. The young unicorn bolted in panic for the thicket.

A horn blared through the dense trees. A thunder of hooves pounded at the end of the glade and Risgan snarled, tightening his fist on his club. A score of horsemen came galloping forth, garbed in a mixture of green leather to ragged furs, shouting and readying bows.

Two other dark shapes veered down from the sky. Shadows of terror to join the existing three isks. With hooked beaks and grasping talons, they dove down upon the riders. The long, moving shadows of their wings stretched far across the glade. One swooped low and raked the foremost horsemen on their helms. They had barely time to nock arrows and take aim. Another marauder smashed a man screaming from his mount while another lifted a man from his saddle and flew westward over the treetops.

The horsemen wheeled about, hurling challenges and brandishing swords. Some scattered as arrows flew. A red-fletched arrow caught the nearest beast in the wing. Risgan raced toward the woman and ducked under a strike of talon, clubbing the offending member, beating its claws back.

The huntress dodged, but not fast enough. The creature clamped talons on her shoulders. It lifted her two feet off the ground and she cried out in pain and dismay.

Risgan staggered with club clutched in hand. The girl was moments away from being lifted forever out of reach! He tossed aside his weapon and grabbed on to its talons before it lifted free. Clinging to a gnarled claw, he purchased firm hold for his life. The woman, white-faced, struggled inches away from him. Jurna smashed his club against the hovering isk's talons before it flew off. Moeze stood a stone's throw away on the grass, rubbing his magic disc. He directed a magical push to thwart the isk. Hape chucked rocks while Kahel nocked another arrow.

Another harsher blare of a horn sounded as the thunder of hooves came closer. "Let me go, you filthy demon!" cried the huntress. She wrenched her bow free as the isk flapped upward. But she could not take proper aim. The beast circled wildly under the club blows and arrows from Jurna and Kahel, trying to lift higher and free, hampered by the reduced power of its injured wing. It strove to shuck Risgan's weight off.

But it could not.

Risgan felt himself buffeted every which way. His world was slipping sideways. Then he caught a mad glimpse of mingled gray sky and earth in his horizon while the awful reek of the bird's hide filled his nostrils. Hanging there desperately, he reached with one hand to snatch at the dagger at his waist. He stabbed again and again into the hard flesh of the exposed leg. The isk gave a hoarse shriek. It loosed its victim. Risgan and huntress fell end over end onto the soft grass.

* * *

Risgan rolled to his knees, shaking the daze out of his skull. He tried to reorient his senses, but nearly collapsed. He reached for the huntress moaning beside him. Dark figures came running. The isk was in the air but a blur in his memory. He struggled to gather his wits. The beast fought, feathers and blood flying every which way, struggling to elude the rain of arrows from the running and mounted figures all around. In a last-ditch attempt for prey, the isk dove and snatched up the young unicorn, confused and looking for its mother, and bore it aloft while the mother limped away, whinnying in distress.

Hape stumbled over to gather the young huntress up.

"Away from her, vagrant," shouted a surly voice on horseback. A wolf-furred man leaped down to kick Hape back, a gleaming, blood-caked sword in hand.

Jurna fumbled for Risgan and managed to haul him to his feet. He shoved the fallen club back into his hands.

A horseman's arrow hit home and the isk gave a screech of

rage. The young foal wriggled out of the isk's grasp and fell in a splayed heap on the ground. But very much alive. The mother gave a whicker of delight and galloped over to gather up her young. Arrows whizzed off in her vicinity despite the isk attack, but fell short of the mark. The hunters vented howls of frustration. The isk was not so lucky and fell under a hail of arrows. Its massive form thudded to the grass. Both wings broken, it flailed around like a beached fish.

The horsemen circled the creature, raining arrows into its feathered hide. A handful of women were among the band. Others jumped down to hack at it with blades.

Surprised at such fury, Risgan watched the riders garbed in worn leathers and steel caps vent their rage. The lead hunter who had spoken the harsh warning to Hape wore a crude wolf fur cape draped about his massive shoulders. His black boots were heavy with mud and he wore a great scowl on a scarred face. Dusty brown hair hung down to his waist under a gleaming helm. His hand lay not far from bow and broadsword at his side. His cap looked more polished than the others and was dressed with feathers and makeshift wolf ears. A band of his other wild horsemen wheeled about, guarding more of the same feverish look in their eyes as each warily scanned the sky. But no more of the beaked marauders came. The surviving isks dwindled to specks then disappeared over the willowy treetops.

Risgan paused to assess his wounds and those of his companions. Aside from cuts and bruises, remarkably they had emerged unscathed.

A druid approached on a black stallion adorned with a blanket dyed blood-red and woven with designs of stags and unicorns on its borders. A single antler horn rose from a conical cap of copper color that contrasted to a gray staff clutched in his gnarled right fist.

Another horseman rode up behind, having the haughty mien of a tribal chief. The multi-hued emblem of a stag dueling on its hind legs with a unicorn adorned his leather jerkin. A signification of rank? Risgan could not tell. He swayed on his feet. The chief hopped off his mount and gathered the young woman up in his arms. "Arcadia, child! We thought you were lost. Are you hurt?"

"Nothing but a few bruises and sprains, Father." She wiped her brow and grimaced, pawing the grime off her leathers. Her chest heaved. Her tousled brown curls hung in disarray. Grass stains and a bloody crimson cut marred her bruised cheek, but she still looked as lovely as ever. Perhaps even more so now after witnessing her brave show and fighting spirit. The chief signaled to the horsemen to bring water and cloth to cleanse her shoulder and wrap the wound.

One of the green-vested riders reined in his black mare and jumped down to attend her. "Arcadia! What on earth has happened?" Pushing forward, he clasped her arms—a handsome youth with striking physique and long dark hair tucked under a peaked hunter's cap. His face creased in distress, his cheeks flushed and gleaming with sweat. "Why did you run off? We were worried sick." His sword hung scabbarded at his hip, along with a curious-looking golden arrow which caught Risgan's attention.

Arcadia lifted a hand to wipe her split lip. "I saw a movement at the edge of the forest. I broke away from the hunting party, thought it an unusual looking stag. For some reason I felt compelled to follow it. Then I saw it was not a stag but a unicorn! I could not believe I almost killed it. Rather than frighten it, I stayed very still…to my delight…it came to me."

The hetman, Arcadia's father, responded in a scolding tone. "That was foolish. The woods are dangerous places, child. As that isk is testament. Never do that again."

She winced in frustration. "I'm sick of your men, Father. Always dogging my heels as if I'm a child. I've already lived sixteen years. I want to hunt on my own. You follow me around like a nanny."

"Better that than have you in the belly of an isk," the hetman grumbled.

She gave a rebellious toss of her head, then looked away.

The leader of the wild horsemen jumped off his snorting mare and struck the young huntsman a reeling blow on the face. It knocked him backward. "Get away from her, you fool! She's mine. You possessed the golden arrow. Why did you not shoot?"

The huntsman, lean and wiry, shrugged off the unexpected blow and bent to steady the maiden whom he had jostled. His long, loose green-leather jerkin was in direct contrast to the stinking furs of the man who had slugged him. The horseman snatched the golden arrow from the younger man's hip before he could object.

Risgan's eyes widened at the sight of the diamond tip on the golden arrow. As any relic hunter's would. Before the huntsman could lay hands on it, the lead horseman tossed it to the druid who gazed down with stern judgment from his horse.

"My lord Mygar, I—" The young hunter stammered.

"What? Spit it out, fool!"

"I could not harm Arcadia, sir. The foreigner was clinging to the isk's talons. If I risked a shot, he might have fallen— lightening the load, allowing the isk to fly out of range—"

Mygar, the lead horseman, cast him a stony glare. "If Arcadia, the hetman's own daughter and my bride to be, were carried off by the barbaric thing, you think her fate ripped apart by the savage beast's brood would have been any better?"

"My lord—"

Mygar struck the young hunter again. "You sniveling simpleton!"

"Leave him alone," cried Arcadia, surging forward.

The druid nudged his horse past Risgan to intercede. "I will point out that Arcadia's life has been spared by the providence of the gods…Somehow in the form of this foreigner's intervention, not Lokbur's indecision."

"Bollocks! Nothing but priestly rhetoric," Mygar cried. "He's a coward and a bungling fool." The cluster of wild horsemen huffed in agreement while they rode around the group in a circle while the green-vested men of Arcadia's clan grumbled.

"Enough! Blame is useless at this late hour," called the hetman. "One warrior has been carried off to his doom and several nurse injuries. The black-feathered beast will take the victim to some foul eyrie in the hinterlands, likely from there slowly rip him apart to feed its younglings."

Risgan looked down at the dead bird. Its black-feathered fury was quenched forever, its yellow eyes glazed in death. The isks were mean killers with the black face and long gray beak of the wild rook. But many times larger, and sported the dull, yellow eyes of the predatory great gray owl. Although he'd encountered many isks in his travels, avoiding many close scrapes with them, he'd never gotten used to the baleful, yellow eyes that could mesmerize a man. Scavengers, slayers and butchers. Making falcons and eagles seem as tame as quail.

Mygar flourished an accusing hand. "Likely you rogues attracted the isks and almost got Arcadia killed."

Jurna growled in anger. "'Twas nothing like that."

"Who's this vagrant then who was reaching for her?"

"His name's Hape. I'm Risgan and this is Jurna the

Journeyman. There's Kahel the Archer. We are wayfarers, nothing more. Hape only intended to assist her to her feet."

"Do not forget me, Moeze, your practicing magician," piped up Moeze.

"Magician, eh? So you say." Mygar glowered. "You seem a suspicious lot."

The hetman climbed on his horse and trotted forward to gaze upon them with undisguised puzzlement. "Who are these men, Mygar? I did not catch their titles."

"Wayfarers, they say." He snorted. "A load of bollocks, if you ask me. Look at their soiled and tattered cloaks. They smell like a pack of sewer rats. Probably down-of-luck bandits who haven't bathed in weeks."

The hetman stroked his chin. "No doubt. They do look like thieves and bandits on a mission. But their part in this debacle is still under question."

"I say we roast them," threatened another of Mygar's hunters, a ragged bully with squinting eye and spittle pooling in the black gap in his front teeth.

The young man, Lokbur, who had been struck moved to soothe the hetman's daughter, despite Mygar's venomous leer. "Are you okay? How fare you? Did these men harm you?"

Arcadia shook her head. "They're not bandits. This one here is a brave man. All of them are. If they hadn't—I would be—" she trailed off, swallowing hard "—I would have been the one carried off along with Gronjil. They have strong magic. A tree split in two. It startled the isk."

The hetman frowned. "That seems an odd, if stupid thing to do, child—you could have been crushed by the tree—making them only more guilty of this mess."

Moeze stirred, raised his disc in a curt manner. "Take care, lord, lest I weave a spell to coat your bearded chin with a golden

17

itch. You cannot slander us so easily."

The hetman's cheeks flushed red. "An insolent mouth have you, magician."

Risgan winced, glared at the mage and signaled Kahel to elbow Moeze in the ribs.

"Agreed, lord," said Risgan. "The stripling is but green in the art of statecraft. Somewhat junior also in spell-casting."

"In what capacity do you serve?" the hetman demanded.

"I am Chief Risgan—leader of this small band, a hunting band like yourselves, on an expedition from Zanzuria, my homeland. Our travels have taken us far and wide. Suffice it to say, game has been scarce. Hunger and losing our way brought us to this glade where we spotted your daughter and hoped to ask for directions."

"Indeed, judging from your impoverished looks that might explain some mysteries. I am Thäene Vardot, 33rd hetman of the Caerlin Clan, 20th chief of the Vithibri Tribe." The words rolled off his tongue a little too pompously for Risgan's tastes. "You've crossed into our hunting territory—a trespass of serious consequence."

"We only wish to pass through your lands in peace," assured Risgan.

"Point taken." The hetman sighed. "It is too late for last wishes though."

Moeze stepped up to assert himself. "I am senior magician of the—the Crystal Circle—and demand to be heard." He stabbed a thumb to his chest in affirmation.

The druid sputtered to contain his disbelief. "That is preposterous. Only seasoned wizards can exhibit magic. Yours is nothing but fledgling magic. Seize the swine!"

Risgan fluttered his fingers. "My humble associate apologizes for his indiscretion. He is young, lord. You can't fault him for his ineptitude. He's just learning."

The hetman held up a hand. "I'm afraid it's more complicated than that, Risgan. Your crimes number in the many. Interrupting a Thäene's sacred hunt, jeopardizing the safety of a hetman's daughter, trespassing on clan property. Repercussions are in order."

Risgan creased his brow. He chewed his lip at the litany of accusations while Kahel fumed, baring his teeth at Moeze and fingering his bow. A murderous look crawled over his scarred face. Jurna stifled a yawn; pale-faced Hape visibly shuddered.

Mygar raised an impatient fist. "Enough of this charade! I say we take out our grievance on these louts—in blood and coin. How much gold do you have on you?"

Risgan scowled. "Not much, I'm afraid."

"Then blood it is! Strip them, lads—of garments and weapons."

"Stand back," threatened Kahel, raising his bow. He aimed at Mygar's breast.

"Now look what you've done," hissed Risgan. He shouldered Moeze aside.

Moeze gave a helpless shrug.

"Leave them alone!" Arcadia cried. She leapt in to defend the outnumbered band. Men from both sides hesitated and looked to Mygar and the hetman for further direction.

Risgan blinked in astonishment. Heaven help Mygar, as fierce as he was, if he were to try to tame this wild fox. Upon closer inspection, he could see Arcadia's soft leather was of the finest quality, a hunter's green for camouflage. Her vibrant brown curls were thick and luxuriant and fell every which way in not unattractive patterns down her slender back. It left her quite stunning in her trim garb. But not entirely dismissible was the stubbornness and fire that lurked under the surface of her flushed face.

One of the few young mounted women had ridden up to listen to the talk and sighed as she spoke, "Sister, you are always the defiant one." The woman's chest rose and fell and she raked over Risgan a sultry, calculating glance that seemed to contain more than a hint of approval. Risgan returned the look with an appraising nod of his own.

"Says the scorched kettle to the boiled-over pot," Arcadia muttered.

"Enough!" cried the hetman. "You two shall not square off here." He waved a weary hand. "Today is a sacred day for the hunt. We must salvage what we can. The rest of the matter will be decided back in Caerlin. You men will come with us!" He waved his heavily-jeweled hand at Risgan and his comrades.

The lead huntsman prodded them along. "Come on, all of you!"

* * *

Things were not looking up for Risgan and his band. More mounted hunters had joined the company. Some went on ahead while five remained to encircle and guard the prisoners.

Risgan looked back to see Mygar's men hacking the head off the fallen isk as a trophy and leaving its steaming entrails strewn on the grass. Grumbling men milled about, stewing about the loss of their fellow hunter. "We'll conduct ceremony for him back at the village," muttered Mygar. "'Tis an unexpected loss."

"Perhaps it will appease your bloodthirsty god," suggested the druid.

"It should have been me," murmured Arcadia.

Lokbur stared aghast. "Don't say that, Arcadia. Nobody should have died." He hung his head. "I feel responsible for this. Had I fired the magic arrow—"

"Do not blame yourself, Lokbur," Arcadia soothed. "'Twas

I who snuck off from the hunt, compelled by a whim." She flashed him a disarming smile and touched his trembling hand. There passed a faint but brief look of intimacy between the two, then it was gone in the blink of an eye. Arcadia mounted her horse, the reins of which one of the other clansmen had handed her.

The woman's watery eyes and trembling lip told of the shambles of the day. "At least the unicorns escaped." The curved longhorn bow hung slack at her side. She stared at Risgan. "Despite your noble intentions, wayfarer, your deeds have stirred up more unrest in our broken clan than ever."

"And if it wasn't for Kahel's arrows and Risgan's heroics, you'd be deader than the isk," pointed out Jurna.

She looked away, but with a sniff of reflection.

Risgan turned at a flutter of movement from the brush. A white tail flashed among the twitch trees.

"The unicorn has returned!" one of Mygar's men cried. "After it!" A host of horsemen spurred forth to chase the creature down, their bows drawn and swords lifted.

Kahel shook his head. "What animal in its right mind would be dumb enough to linger here?"

"It's no unicorn," Risgan said.

A priest beside the druid reined his horse forward to stop them. "Driadis curse you all," he shouted. He waved his staff. "The old gods will rise in their graves to haunt those for molesting their sacred animals."

Mygar trotted forth to face down the priest. "What do you plan to do about it, knave?"

"Out of my way," the priest snarled. "Somebody has to defend the traditional ways." He turned to smack the insolent chief across the head with his staff but landed a stroke on the shoulder instead.

Mygar grinned and leaned in, raising his broadsword. The druid's staff came down again and Mygar blocked it with his blade. This time he leaned in to smash his gloved fist into the priest's face. The priest slid to the ground, dazed and gasping.

"Uncle, no!" cried Arcadia, hurrying forth.

Mygar spat on him. "I say that Wülv, our fanged wolf god, fine spirit he is, spits on the old gods. 'Tis the head of Wülv with his hoary wolf ears and slavering jowl that adorns your shit altars and fanes now, not that feeble teat-sucking Driadis."

One of the green-leathered men gave a fierce cry and galloped in to avenge the vicious sacrilege. The gesture caught Mygar by surprise and angered as he was at being struck, he mustered a wild swing and parried the bold thrust, then he reversed the sword and ran the rider through. He slid out of the saddle with a cry and a thud.

Arrows trained on each other from both sides. The ragged men looked to their hetman for a signal to attack.

Vardot merely looked away, lip quivering. Mygar's eyes gleamed with derisive intensity. Arcadia knelt to console her uncle, holding him in her arms.

"Remember Driadis, my child," the priest croaked. "Dark times are upon us. Pray to the goddess Driadis." He wheezed out a bloody gasp, then looked at his hands where blood flowed from his broken nose.

"Anybody else have a bone to pick?" challenged Mygar.

Arcadia lunged forward with a strident shriek, her sword sweeping out in a killing arc. Mygar parried her blade, then jumped down to face her, his grin ever wider. "Come on, my bonny lass, that's no way to treat your future husband."

The clash of steel echoed through the glade as she surged in to strike him down. The huntress chopped and slashed and Mygar defended his ground. The wicked smirk continued to crease his leathery face as the two swords cried out with each parry. He put one insolent hand on his hip and defended, stroke for stroke, with blade clutched in the other.

"Ah, a spirited wench is what I want to warm my bed! Can't you do better than that, Arcadia?" He leaped aside, then dodged her vicious swing as she turned to spit full in his face.

"Stop this nonsense!" her father bellowed.

Arcadia ignored her father's outburst. She drove in ever more furiously.

Gutsy mettle this maiden showed, Risgan thought, as he watched in admiration. She displayed skills beyond her years, a natural at the blade. But Mygar was faster, and slier, and ever more experienced and meaner. He twisted on his heels and snuck inside her guard and brought his gloved hand down on hers, ripping the sword from her grasp. With a grunt he tossed it away into the bushes. He stared at her, eyes fuming. Then he bowed. "Very nice, milady. We should do this dance more often."

"You disgusting brute," she spat.

"And so complimentary."

She sprang at him, teeth bared and nails outstretched.

He caught her by the wrists then flung her away. "Deal with her, Vardot! Do you hear me?"

The hetman hissed and signaled two of his men. They came running in to restrain Arcadia, despite her mortified cries. "Let me go, you stupid fools! Who is the enemy here?"

Several looked to Vardot for a signal to attack Mygar, but the hetman just shook his head. A sigh rippled through the gathering. The druid looked on with a face of stone.

Vardot sat atop his mount, teeth clenched. "Have you enough bullying for one day, Mygar? You've killed one of my men and maimed my under-priest. Are you satisfied?"

"Very much. There will be more violence if you don't heed my warning and show some respect and control your vixen of a daughter. Isks fly and the hunt is not yet over! Onward!" he barked at his hunters. "The hunt for game must continue!"

The horsemen returned from the thickets, admitting that they had found no sign of a unicorn. The hetman's green-clad men groaned in disgust. They gathered up the fallen horseman and the wounded priest.

At that moment another horn blared through the trees. A clot of new figures came charging into the glade—more of Mygar's company by the look of them: lean-jawed, heavy-muscled, steel-capped men dressed in furs and leathers.

"News, lord," cried the leader, a tall, sinewy man with bronze rings on his arms. He drew abreast of Mygar. "A pack of stags run loose in Falgron's glade. Jorgu, the old marksmen, got a piece of one—" His mouth dropped upon sight of the carnage. "What in the name of wild Wülv has gone on here?"

"Never mind." Mygar gave him a brisk flourish. "We'll be moving out of here soon, Svengar. Prepare your men—the wolf-hunters." Cheers of enthusiasm coursed from the fur-cloaked hunters.

"Guard this popinjay, well," hissed Mygar, pointing the tip of his sword at Risgan. "My horsemen and I will deal with him and the others when I'm back."

Svengar grumbled. "As you wish, lord."

"They will have a proper trial," warned the hetman.

Mygar shrugged and gave a harsh laugh. "They'll feel the bite of my sword, is what." He turned and raised his blade to the sky. "The hunt goes on!" Springing upon the back of his horse, a broad-chested brown bay, he rallied his wild hunters. They roared in answer and turned to speed off.

Arcadia raised a shrill cry: "Not so fast! We must look after our wounded. The animal totems speak that—"

Mygar reined in, peering at her with narrowed eyes. "What do you know about animals and their spirits, woman? I've spent twice your years herding them and killing them, and wandering about these wilds like a priest of the hunt."

"I know more than you think, Mygar."

"Hear, hear," cried the green-vested men of Arcadia's clan. The other wild horsemen, savages of Mygar's clan, jeered in opposition.

Risgan's brain spun with the wide schism in this group. Half were for appeasing Arcadia, half against. Grumbles of dissent rang like deerhide drums. The hetman's face clouded over.

As the remainder prepared to leave, another cry came. Those of the hetman's green-vests brought the cart forth carrying an agitated Afrid.

"What manner of loathsome creature is this?" the hetman demanded.

"Thäene Vardot, meet Afrid, erstwhile witch of Thornkeep," Risgan said. He made the introduction with a low, mocking bow.

Afrid hissed.

"You don't say?" The hetman gaped. "Her reputation precedes her. 'Tis' a spiteful crone I see, with a baby's face."

"Agreed."

Even the antlered druid had trotted forward to grant Afrid a more careful inspection. Though it looked as if he liked little of what he saw.

The hetman gave a weary sigh. "Tolfgard! Mesin! Bring the witch along with us. They shall all return with us to the village. Let us make haste!"

* * *

So the hunt proceeded without incident, though Risgan

watched the hetman and the small band of Mygar's hunters scour the skies with wary eyes. Only three stags did they flush out from the thick brush, beasts whose carcasses were well pierced and slung over the backs of spare horses. Risgan's mouth watered for venison roasting over a crackling fire, but he knew that was a pipe dream.

The huntsmen designated as guards drove Risgan and his company hard through the wilds. The peeling gray bark and thin wispy branches became a blur in his mind. Finger-like twigs scratched his cheeks and caught at his leathers. The natural alleys and corridors through the hag birch and twitchwood grew dim in the coppery light as Arcadia rode alongside them, flashing them occasional glances, as if pitying their ignoble treatment. "It's not normal this happens," she said to Risgan. "It won't be long now. Our village is but a half hour away."

"That's good to know," Risgan said, loosing a noisy breath. The hetman trotted ahead with his clansmen in a dark mood. His uncommunicative druid rode at his side, while Mygar and his wolf-furred hunters ranged off elsewhere to hunt. Only ten of Mygar's guard stayed behind to watch the hetman and his prisoners, but that was enough. The chief's subjects also watched Risgan and his company closely. Risgan made note of Jurna's itchy fingers on his sword and Kahel's gleaming eyes as if they contemplated an escape. At this point it was folly and he jabbed an elbow into Kahel's ribs, warning him that impulsive action would lead to death, surrounded as they were by the horsemen's drawn bows.

Dark billowy clouds moved in from the north. By late afternoon all the golden light had disappeared from the sky as they neared a freshwater river. The arms of the forest opened up to look out upon brooding flats where a long low salt marsh spread. Deadheads rose among the mire. A bridge provided access over the sluggish stream that emptied into the marsh.

A wooden wall surrounded two sides of the village with trees and water on the other sides. Archers poised above the entrance gate, bows at the ready. The gate swung open; the horses trotted through.

A group of longhouses lined the river while bull reeds and pussy willows sprung up near the shore. Hale, leather-clad women and eager children came out to greet the hunters.

The day was still warm, not much wind so midges swarmed; a faint reek accompanied what breeze there was, bringing the waft of rotten vegetation and human waste.

Odd place for a settlement, Risgan thought.

The hunters dismounted and hung the spoils of the hunt from branches to drain them of their blood. Other carcasses looked to have hung there for some time and were pulled down for the communal feast, soon to be roasted over fires. It was a good thing, for Risgan's belly ached with hunger. In the meantime, the hetman ordered bowls of broth brought for the riders to tide over their hunger.

While they gulped the offerings, Risgan noticed a scout hawk circling overhead whose lone piercing cry rang shrill in the late afternoon. It scattered the other birds in the twitchwood and flew down toward the hunters. Where were the dogs to help them hunt? He asked as much to the gathered hunters and one of the Caerlineans replied,

"Dogs make short work of game. Their teeth tear into the spoils before we can get there."

Risgan blinked. "Makes sense."

"Train them then," said Kahel.

"Easier to make pigs fly. At least the dogs in these parts."

Jurna grunted. "Your king seems to enjoy the likes of hunts and horses and hawks. I'd have thought he'd make hounds part of his retinue."

"We have no king, only a hetman."

"So we've heard," growled Kahel.

To the side of the common ground facing the huts loomed a hulk of scorched, blackened stone which looked something like a temple or monastery.

"That's Driadis's Sanctuary," said one of the hunters. "Or what's left of it. Burned by invaders. We used to favor the goddess Driadis. Now our druids worship Wülv. We switched to the wolf god at the coming of the outland tribes during the great migration. Their shamans taught us the wisdom of the wolves and eagles, and the importance of the hunt."

Risgan nodded in comprehension. The variety of gods, heroes and animal totems he had seen during his travels had been too numerous to recall. They had come and gone like flies.

A boardwalk stretched out into the salt marsh; in Risgan's estimation a region which sported an eerie gray and unwholesome look. Why they built their village so close to it was a mystery.

The hetman seemed to perceive some of this and inclined his head in a sagely way. "Once this was a swale of fruitful bounty and supported us well. The land was well drained with freshwater creeks. The muskrat competed with the sharp-toothed beaver; both multiplied and dammed the rivers, flooding the area for miles. Even today we cannot control the devils. Every time one of their dams break, two more spring up. Ever do we fear we must leave Caerlin and forge some new settlement. That day will come soon enough. Then there's the marauding isks..." He trailed off, his face pinched in displeasure, perhaps with the foul memory of Arcadia snatched up in grasping claws.

The druid picked up the conversation in a grave voice: "The

isks nest across the great eerie divide in the dead firs beyond the hummocks and hills we call the Swalestrike. Perhaps attracted by the fresh meat." He motioned his hand at the squalid village and gave a bitter laugh. "Even their greedy talons and slavering beaks cannot cull the beavers. We keep sharp lookout for the isks and from time to time they carry off our children when our hunters are engaged. Even though we despise them, they are sacred birds.

Risgan frowned. "These isks seem a menace not worth the risk."

"'Twas not always like this." He sighed. "They used to be mighty protectors. Hasifer the Traitor played them a trick and incurred their lifelong enmity toward humans and thus an everlasting curse."

"Indeed," said Risgan.

"What...you question our lore?" the druid snapped.

"Nothing like that." Risgan held up a hand. "I merely assert that being a man of the world, having hunted fabled treasures far and wide, my very existence depends largely on the truth of such legends."

"Is that so?" The hetman's words echoed hollowly.

Upon explicit orders, the horse guards took Risgan and company to a spacious but gloomy hall within a large wooden longhouse. Timber beams supported a high ceiling. A hearth stood at the side, now cold with ashes. An elderly judge with white hair and a visible stoop bent clearing the ash and coughed at the sight of them. "Thäene Vardot, Arcadia, welcome." He bowed. "I trust the hunt was a success."

"Indeed it was."

"I see you have brought back some friends."

The hetman nodded curtly. He gave a quick summary of the isk attack, the casualties, the near escape of Arcadia, and the presence of the unicorns and outlanders whom he introduced one by one.

The judge rubbed his chin. "I see. Present their cases then—" he gave a long sigh, as if dreading the thought of hearing five defenses in one day.

Risgan and company were allowed to say their part, then Arcadia gave her account with animated flourishes. After much haranguing and questioning back and forth, the hetman called order to the assembly. "Judge Kjarn. What is your verdict?" He paused. "Wait, I want to hear it in private first."

They repaired to the antechamber and both returned, the hetman wearing a brief scowl. "After listening to Judge Kjarn's esteemed opinion, I concur that action must be taken."

The hetman, his round face flushed, lifted a finger to lips and gave a sharp exhalation, "Risgan, seeing as your company inadvertently trespassed on our ancestral lands and provoked an isk attack which almost lost me my daughter, I sentence you and your men to hunt down and kill fifteen stags of excellent quality in the upcoming hunts. Three for each member of your party."

Risgan choked on his tongue. "What? This punishment seems excessive. Clearly we are innocent of any crimes."

Arcadia leaped to her feet. "I too, Father, must object. Risgan was instrumental in saving my skin. You heard my testimony."

The hetman held up his hand. "Is that ingratitude I hear? Normally, the punishment for this number of transgressions is severe: a minimum of one year in jail, often accompanied with torture. But in this case, I make an exception, even though these outlanders interrupted a sacred hunt and let a valuable unicorn escape. The adjudicator's word and mine are absolute."

Risgan nodded with a curt growl. "As you wish, Lord. We acknowledge your—leniency." He turned to leave, quelling

Kahel and Jurna's disbelieving stares. He cut off their grumbles with a wink.

"One question," said Moeze, unable to resist the urge. "Can we use sorcery on these hunts to speed up our taking of the fifteen stags?"

The hetman harrumphed. "Ordinarily, no, especially considering your unproven magical skill, Moeze. "In a nutshell, I formally forbid you from exercising any form of magic."

Moeze sputtered but Risgan raised a finger and cautioned the magician to silence. "Young Moeze is most vocal, lord, and for that, I apologize. He accepts your wishes. I will see that he complies."

"A wise choice, Risgan. See that you do."

Risgan drew Moeze aside and hissed. "Fool. Do not annoy the chief any more than you have to. I've told you once and again not to practice magic that involves risk for others. For that matter don't practice magic at all until you are better versed in it and healed from Afrid's vile spells."

Moeze sagged. He hung his head, muttering a terse word. "As you wish, Risgan. In the end it will go the worse for you and the others."

"There is still the matter of this witch." The hetman gestured toward the thorn cage. "The crone exhibits a fiendish aura which disturbs my sensibilities."

Risgan sighed. "Pay no heed. Afrid's suffering penance for her past deeds."

"And what does penance have to do with her sinister aura?" he intoned. "Why the grimacing rictus? The baby face?"

"Trade places and find out," snorted Kahel.

"What's that?" The hetman scowled, noting Kahel's brazen tone, but choosing to bypass it.

Dodonis, Vardot's druid, rubbed his chin. "I might have

uses for such a specimen in the days ahead."

Jurna laughed. "Valuable only as a freak show oddity."

The druid ignored the comment. "I request a transfer of the witch to my hut, Thäene."

Kahel gave a barking laugh. "Go right ahead, druid. She's all yours."

"Not so fast," said Risgan. "Afrid is under my protection and I'll not have her mauled."

Kahel sneered. "When did you become the hag's guardian?"

Vardot called for order. "The caged witch will go to Dodonis for future study! That is the end of the discussion. In the meantime, you can make use of our humble grounds. I'm not an ungenerous man. We have an obstacle course, training ground, workout area, private sparring grounds, baths and a temple to Driadis. Though that now runs with wolf heads. There by the marsh, some fishing piers and equipment are at your service so you can contribute."

"We'll consider it," said Risgan.

The hetman studied them with care. "You'd better. You would do best to offer us service and participate in the training of our hunters, particularly our younger members. Your skills may accelerate your release. Now we have to contend with Mygar's brutes who have moved in on us." He grunted with distaste.

Risgan gave a strangled cough. "Why don't you repel them?"

The chief frowned. "Easier said than done, outlander. They're canny as wolves and immune to ambush. All too well have they become versed in swordsmanship and bullying intimidation."

"And versed in crass behaviors," piped up Arcadia, "as some of our females are well aware of."

Vardot mumbled under his breath. "I know. How I would

love to drive the lot of them into the swamp..." He balled his fists. "We are at their mercy. Nonetheless, they offer protection and hunting skills to our community, so a fragile harmony exists."

"Very fragile, Father—and I wish you'd just—"

"Perhaps there is something you can offer," the hetman interrupted, toying with his staff. He gazed at Risgan. "If so, the judge may reduce your sentence. We make our young undergo a rigorous practicum to ensure they are fit for the hunt, that they can defend our village from warring tribesmen like these apes who currently control us. Little good our martial skill has availed. Anything you can assist in this regard will be helpful."

"Understandable."

"What is ours is yours, as I have said. But do not try to leave the perimeter of the village. Our guards will repel you, and you'll be punished. Not to mention what Mygar's men will do if they find you have deserted."

Risgan gave a crisp nod. He accepted the situation as it stood.

"Your quarters are being prepared this moment. We have set up accommodations for you in Kevil the blacksmith's longhome. He will billet you."

"That is most kind of you, lord."

He gave a curt nod. "Come, let us prepare for the feast."

With a regal inclination of head he strode away in the direction of the common ground to deal with the many petty issues that every chief had. Squealing pigs, two lame dogs in a fight, a field hand squabbling over a few turnips his neighbor had pulled out. Risgan felt glad that he had not the weight of a chief's duties on his shoulders. Being leader in more than name of this small band was enough of a challenge. Thinking of which, what was he to do about Moeze's infatuation with dangerous and inept spells? They could be the ruin of them all.

Shouts came from the common ground. A scout scurried up, his ruddy face glistening with sweat. "My lord! Terror flies—isks, four of them—they ravage the village!"

"What? Don't just stand there, man, arrow them down!"

He fled back to the battle. On brisk feet the hetman stormed over. Arcadia, Risgan and his band followed close behind.

The common ground writhed to the tune of chaos.

Three giant birds had swooped low, bone-claw talons grasping and raking the straw-thatched huts, tearing holes along their ridges. Villagers ran screaming for their lives. The birds, fast of wing and long of beak, eluded the huntsmen's arrows in the fading light.

"The birds seek vengeance for the death of their brother in the woods!" called one of the huntsmen.

Villagers crouched, wielding blades. Some aimed bows. The arrows skidded off the birds' tough hides. Only a few caught the feathered flesh and stayed lodged, but even those barely deterred the birds' menace. The ten horsemen Mygar had left behind from his company circled on their mounts, drawing the isks out. But their arrows failed to penetrate the tough hide.

Risgan clutched his club, waving it back and forth at the hideous black creature that dove at him all too closely.

"Can you not do anything with your magic, druid?" spat the hetman.

"My lord, the isk is an ancient bird impervious to magic."

"Bollocks! Do something, you fool!"

Arcadia snatched the golden arrow from the druid, who sat atop his horse dazed in inaction. She drew back the strings and it flew in a rainbow arc. The gleaming tip pierced the lead brute in the chest. It gave a ghastly shriek, sagged. Then its massive hulk fell to the ground in a feathery, heap. With wings flapping uselessly on the ground, it crawled along the grass. Miracle upon miracle, the golden arrow emerged of its own volition from the isk's breast and in a looping arc returned through the air back to Arcadia's hand. She strung it again and took aim at a second beast. It swooped to rake her with its talons but Kahel wheeled in and sent a spinning arrow straight into its eye. Lokbur's arrow twanged next, catching it in its side as it careened off in a screeching rage. Villagers came running with angry curses and hoes and axes in their hands, chopping the fallen bird in a frenzy of pent up fury. The beak snapped out and took the legs off one overzealous villager who got too close. He bled out in an instant.

"Kill it, you fools!" the hetman cried.

Jurna stepped up to jam his sword into its beak, silencing the creature's fury forever. Kahel and Lokbur stood at the ready to pepper it with arrows. But the thing moved no more.

"Two attacks in one day. A sinister omen," cried a distraught villager.

In eerie synchrony the other birds swooped low and snatched two huntsmen off their horses and rose aloft from whence they had come.

Risgan stood dumbstruck as the two marauders disappeared into the horizon. A lull descended amid the cries of the wounded. Men's shouts dwindled to angry mutters. Others made slow movements to repair their damaged huts and longhouses.

Lokbur strode up and spoke in fevered words. "Lord Vardot, we will have to launch an offensive against these vile isks sooner rather than later."

"The journey is long and the risk high," asserted the druid.

"Risks we must take, Dodonis," mumbled Vardot. "But not now. Mygar still hunts and we must gather meat and hides for the long winter."

Risgan gazed in wonder upon the hetman's daughter and the fabulous weapon she clutched. Already its diamond tip and shaft grew redder and duskier and seemed to scintillate with an aura of mysterious power. "This arrow you hold, what magic does it possess?"

"Its magic is not fully understood," the druid said.

"And yet even its power is not enough to kill these creatures," scoffed one of Mygar's guards.

Arcadia spoke as if in trance: "It was said the arrow is the trophy of Queen Razastaf who bathed in the magic pool in the woods of the dryads in ancient times. The waters gave her powers of foresight, wisdom beyond her years...and mystical experiences. One day—"

"One day she brought the arrow to her pool and it became ensorcelled," finished Mygar's man. "We've heard the story before."

"She had it fitted with a diamond tip by the best jewel-smiths," continued Arcadia, ignoring the remark. "It sat through the ages until it was stolen from the palace by a Zerulian thief."

"A quaint yarn," scoffed Kahel.

"Yarn or not," contended Jurna. "If not for the courage of this hetman's daughter, we'd be isk bait or weeping tears of blood right now. Seems as if this arrow and a true aim from a maiden's hand saved the day from these vicious creatures."

There came murmurs of agreement.

* * *

The roaring fire blazed amid the grumbles of the villagers, males and females alike, as the huntsmen shared their accounts of the day's happenings and the coming of the unicorns. The druid murmured some prayers in a foreign tongue for the three who had perished. Cedar, sage and wild twitch sprigs hissed and crackled over the fire. The hetman ordered the release of three flaming arrows over the marsh into the deepening dusk.

Heads bowed and a silence was given.

Tables and benches were hauled out and laden with food, bowls and barrels of mead. Some small state of revelry returned to the clans but with extra bows and quivers at hand. Soon after, isk meat roasted over spits and joined the overflowing platters of succulent venison. The trophy head was carried off and tied to a stout post overlooking the glade as a deterrent to other marauders.

"Do you not think it an overly brazen challenge to more of their kind?" asked Risgan, between mouthfuls of meat.

The hetman growled an oath. "'Tis the only thing these foul isks understand. Slaughter and death! So let them feast their eyes on the head of their kin if they return. We'll be ready."

Risgan and members of his band looked upon the mounted head with doubt and wonder. Blood dripped from its severed neck and ran down the dark wood of the post, the sight almost enough to spoil his appetite.

Mygar came riding in with his mob of hunters. He waved his blade, a sneer on his lips. Not a scratch was on him from the dangers of the day. A majestic stag with a top-heavy rack of forked antlers lay stretched over the unsaddled mount tethered behind his own horse.

"Looks as if you fools have lost more men to the beaks of the isks," he called jocularly.

Angry grumbles issued from the Caerlinean hunters.

"And fat lot of good you were," one dared to cry out. "The men you left here were next to useless."

"I cannot be at five places at once," Mygar said. "Can't you weaklings fight your own battles for a change?" He laughed. "Peace! Here's more meat for roasting. Let's make merry and wash our hands of the bloody affairs of the day."

"Not so merry, today, Mygar," called out Arcadia.

He raised an eyebrow. "What's that, my fancy bride-to-be?"

She looked away, fuming, refusing to look at him.

The hetman lifted his cup of wine and made a toast to all gathered. "Four prime stags, four ribbons. That's what is awarded the best hunters of the day. The stag, the symbol of beauty and prosperity, has offered itself for our sustenance. None match its supple grace, save the unicorn." He lifted a ringed finger in the air.

"Except the unicorn," repeated Arcadia, shaking her head. "And these foul brutes would have killed them all and made doormats of them."

Risgan nodded, commiserating with Arcadia's frustration.

Mygar merely shrugged.

Ale guzzling competitions were soon in full swing, starting early this evening. Risgan motioned to one of Mygar's bearded rogues, Svengar who was laughing, downing a huge jack of ale that spilled foam down his jerkin. "Who are these dolts? Where did they come from? I don't like the look of them. Here in your village they are like sharks among minnows."

Arcadia expelled an angry breath. "They're not part of our clan as my father explained. They just think they are. They came from the east a year ago, hooligans and warmongers. Expelled from their own clan, the Svengari, following a blood feud. Mygar rallied them; he assumed leadership. He came to us all blood-smeared and yelling in his foul tongue, a fierce, uncouth barbarian. Since then, he has installed himself here with his wolves as our 'protectors'. Pah! He rules and my father is nothing more than a puppet. That bastard over there to his left is his lieutenant and nephew, Svengar, a man as mean as a rattler. His uncle obviously taught him everything he knows."

Risgan peered over at Svengar, a sinewy brute with bronze warrior rings on his arms and hair like his uncle's down the middle of his back. Though this was dirty blond with a dyed strip of black, it had no less menace and denoted a rising champion of the hunters.

Mygar and he clasped hands.

"And the druid?"

"Dodonis is halfway between the two, my father and Mygar. He's split between the old ways and the new. Ever looking for a chance to grab at some power and opportunity at the expense of anyone who gets in the way.

"A pack of thieves and vipers," Risgan muttered. "Your tale sheds more light on the situation at least."

Lokbur came by to pay his respects to Arcadia. His face had a red welt which he tried to hide in an awkward fashion. He seemed almost shame-faced about it.

"Arcadia." He tipped his head with a forced smile.

"Lokbur. I thank you for coming to my defense back there."

He nodded grimly and looked at her with obvious fondness. "Ever am I watching out for you, huntress. Seems you're a magnet for trouble." He gave a tense laugh. "Remember the time you got into the bee hives a few years back, licking your fingers of honey? Ha. Oh, what a mess that was. How many villagers got stung?"

She chuckled. "Too many. I remember well, Lokbur. All just follies of a rebellious childhood. Remember when we used to hold hands by the river? I fell in and you rescued me. You pulled me out by the hair and I smacked you good, if I recall. We'd talk for hours, catch fish in the sun, then bask in the shade, sometimes even sneak a kiss, or two."

"I remember." He grinned and blushed with clear enjoyment of the moment from the past. "We were not even twelve or thirteen." His eyes glazed over and grew bright and dreamy at their shared memories. Then they dimmed, as if such things were only ghosts of yesterday. "And yet, thirteen is an unlucky number."

His voice was drowned out by the drunken whoopings of the wolf-hunters. "We got four stags today, not a bad haul, but could be better," clamored one.

Risgan murmured under his breath, "Pity to slay such magnificent beasts."

The hunter, one of Mygar's rogues, overheard the remark and gave an angry shout. "Who are you to make a judgment on us, outlander? Would you rather eat turnips tonight?" Others laughed.

Risgan shrugged. "I was merely appreciating the majesty of the beasts."

"And the isks are majestic and we slay them too."

This raised jeers. The fur-cloaked wolf-hunters catcalled.

Dodonis the druid spoke in a commanding tone, waving his staff. "The unicorn leathers and hide are magical and essential for our charms and spells."

Svengar flashed Risgan a contemptuous glance, "I say we slay these knaves, as Mygar suggests."

Others of Mygar's band voiced their agreement.

"Silence your tongues," the hetman called. "They have undergone a proper trial and are under my protection."

"You forget," said Mygar in a quiet voice, "we don't obey you." He approached, his eyes glassy with mead, somewhat placated by the spoils of the day. He lifted a hand. "Peace, comrades. It is a time of feasting and celebration!—didn't you hear?" he roared, slurring his words, "your 'chief' has said it himself, a sacred day for the hunt. The outlanders will live—for now!" He raised his sword high and cast Risgan an evil look.

Risgan bared his teeth, not liking what he saw.

"Brute," hissed Arcadia. She turned her head aside.

Traditional wrestling matches began, accompanied by music with lute and drum and other instruments that Risgan had not heard before. Some with long hollow cylinders carved of wood and a place for a musician to blow into.

Caerlin clansman built a second bonfire that soared up into the black night, dispelling the gloom and chill of the change of season. Children ran freely, wearing hats and eye-patches, playing blind man's bluff, with Arcadia playing monkey in the middle—all to the delight of the children. She even got her sister to join in, then Jurna and Hape. Others played a variation of hide and seek while rowdier youths bobbed for apples in barrels filled to the brim. Moeze went even so far as to demonstrate a magic trick or two, but Risgan came up behind him and offered a cock-eyed smile and whispered in his ear. "Moeze, I know you like to impress the children, but stick to the disappearing bead under the three-cups-trick, okay?"

The magician frowned at him, then smiled. "Yes, Risgan, simpler is better." He tapped his chin. "And yet, this is not what I expected—but certainly better than taking residence in Afrid's lair. Speaking of which, I wonder how our hag is faring?"

Risgan gave a brief mutter. "As you witnessed, she has been confined to the druid's hut. Douran only knows what he will do with her. Frankly, part of me is relieved to have her off my hands. I only hope the idiot does not let her escape."

"Aye, pray that he does not," said Jurna.

Kahel lifted a cup of mead to his lips and drained it in a single gulp. "Bah, this is mere goat piss! I've tasted stronger water than this."

Arcadia laughed. "Let's see you say that after twenty more cups, archer."

"Why, mistress? You challenging me?" he chuckled.

"Judging from your size and capacity, no."

Kahel smiled, a rare act for him.

Musicians brought out deerhide drums while others clutched lute and fife and started up a lively tune that had many tapping their feet. A chorus of singers joined in. The village folk kicked up their heels and danced around the fire. A high-spirited mood had them striking up a jig that involved deep knee bends with hands on hips and high-flinging kicks. Risgan chanced to make eye contact with the lady Thrulia, the hetman's older daughter who watched with some interest. With a shrug, he sauntered over, knowing he had nothing to lose. So, he put on his best smile, eager to start up a conversation.

"Lady Thrulia," he said with a bow. "We have not formally met. I'm Risgan, a relic hunter of small repute."

"Pleased to meet you." She lifted her had in offer. "Shall we dance?" He accepted and they promenaded with the others around the fire.

"You have the look of an adventurer to you," she remarked. "The fit, wiry type with a dash of sandy-haired mystique thrown in. It speaks of mischievousness. I'm a good judge of men...Those vagabondish leathers of yours—they have the looks of an outlaw."

Risgan shrugged. "Others have said as much."

She nodded. Perhaps a handful of years older than Arcadia, Risgan guessed, but she exhibited the same fiery spirit, the same bright inquiring green eyes, and slender figure, though she was not as tall, but no less striking.

"You are an odd sort, Risgan. You have the gentlemanly quality of an older man, yet the look of a far younger one."

"It's an odd combination," Risgan said, bowing again. "I take pride in my upbringing at an early age."

"Oh? And from where do you come that demands such upbringing?"

"Zanzuria." He grinned. "A fiefdom several leagues distance. Perhaps you've heard of it?"

She nodded. "In name only."

"A proud kingdom ruled by a proud man. Although sometimes I wonder who rules: him or his queen." He chuckled.

"Lady Farella is quite a handful—from what I've gathered."

"Oh, she is."

"Zanzuria...one of the old kingdoms, blessed with an opulent palace and elegant gardens. One day I hope to see it and experience its charms. Our humble village of Caerlin, as you can see, is not much to speak of." She arched her back. "But— it's not often that a woman rules a kingdom, is it?"

"Farella is a spirited maid."

"More than I?" she asked in a playful voice.

Risgan spun about. He lifted his long legs in one of the scissor kicks demanded of the dance. "I do not like to compare women. Not very gentlemanly, you see."

She chuckled. "Don't shove your foot deeper into the mire, sir Risgan. Let's just enjoy our dance."

"Of course." Risgan was relieved to drop the conversation, which he found bordering on stressful, considering the carnal nature of his liaisons with the lady Farella, which Thrulia seemed so cunningly to have guessed.

Thrulia's long rose-colored hair gleamed in the crackling flames. How he would like to stroke it. The flushed faces of the dancers mooned around them. Risgan tried an innovation to the 'kick' which earned her laughter and everyone's admiration.

"You seem quite adept at those high jumps and kicks."

"And I no less envious of your dexterity, milady."

"Indeed, have you danced the *riga* before?"

"No, this is my first time."

She sputtered out a laugh. "Of course."

She drew in close and gripped his waist and spun him around.

Risgan stumbled, surprised at the bold maneuver. But he quickly recovered and echoed the move, grinning and twirling her with more force than she expected. Was she testing his mettle? When she landed on her feet and turned back to face him, she was slightly breathless. He grabbed her and tossed her high in the air. Wild cheers rose from the spectators, many of whom had stepped back to observe and give them more space.

"Well, wasn't that fun?" he asked with a broad, disarming grin. "But you, lady, you have not said much of yourself."

Thrulia shrugged. "What is there to say, sir Risgan? I am a hetman's daughter, no more, no less. Destined to become some poor huntress like my sister, though I'll never be as good as her. Likely my father will wed me to some savage boor like that thuggish, lank-toothed Svengar over there. See how he watches me with an obnoxious leer pasted on his ugly face. He makes my skin crawl."

Risgan's head turned as the dance steps slowed and indeed he saw the chief's lieutenant crouched with his bearded cronies over grogs on tree stumps for tables, eyeing the women with lascivious interest and trading rude jests.

Risgan's expression grew somber. "I'd rather see all hell freeze over than you wed to that mongrel."

She grinned. "That is sweet of you to say. Yet somewhat of an inevitability. As it is, I feel sick at heart knowing that Arcadia must become bride to that savage brute of a chief." She shivered at the thought. "Even the rebel that she is, he'll break her spirit."

"Can nothing be done?"

She frowned; a pained look surfaced on her comely face. "And what would you have us do, Risgan—declare open war on these animals? They'd tear us apart. We must appease them, as my father has stated."

He grunted, pondering this defeatist attitude. He missed another step and almost pitched himself into the fire. He regained control and faced her with a faint smile. A fight lost was better than slavery. But what could he do? Leave them to blunder along with their own battles? For the moment, he'd watch and wait and enjoy these halcyon moments with this captivating maid while he had the chance.

Mygar, inebriated, staggered about, his hair askew, deliberately dancing with every female in the two clans but his future bride. Perhaps to spite her? It suited the hetman's daughter just fine. She sat out and rebuffed all dance partners save Lokbur.

The dance came to an end; sudden loud shouts erupted from a disorderly cluster of Mygar's huntsmen as another fight broke out, apparently over who claimed title to the last stag slain in the hunt. Mygar allowed it, even encouraged it, punishing the loser with a cane-whipping. Risgan and his men were not alone in their sullen misgivings about this rowdy clan.

The hour grew late and even more boisterous tumult echoed from the Svengari huntsmen, though many had returned to their squalid camp next to the village on the shores of the swamp. Risgan, enlivened by the dance and a growing passion for Thrulia, drowned himself in grog. There seemed to be no end. The hypnotic voices of Jurna and Moeze blurred together in a background hum of boasts and threats, the clash of swords in mock battles becoming one; all the while the two bonfires continued to burn as the raucous music progressed to the rhythmic beat of drums, and whistling and wheezing of multiple wind instruments accompanied by the drunken singing of ribald verses decidedly off key, until Risgan had finally had enough.

He and his crew stumbled back to the blacksmith's longhome and flung themselves on the dusty blankets slung out in front of the hearth. The fire had long grown cold. After a time, the master of the house came stumbling bleary-eyed upon them where they snored away. Risgan sprang upright at the sound of the blacksmith's sandal scuffling on the dirt.

"Sorry sir, not my wish to wake you," the blacksmith apologized. "Just wanted to check everything was alright."

Risgan nodded and yawned. Likely not checking on their comfort for altruistic purposes. Rather, verifying that they hadn't made off with his valuables, despite the assurances of the hetman that they were not thieves or murderers. "Quite alright, master Kevil. I always sleep with one eye open."

The blacksmith wandered back to his quarters with a doubtful glance over his shoulder. Trust, it seemed, was not easily gained in this village.

2: The Magic Arrow

After a hurried breakfast of hot meal and oatcakes, Kevil hustled Risgan and his gang off to the fringes of the village. "Where are we going?" Risgan asked.

"You'll see. Hetman's orders." The dawn's pearly light filtered through the trees to pierce the mist and glaze the trampled grass a washed-out silver. On cresting a small rise, Risgan stared with some awe upon a tall palisade with stout, close-set poles—a gigantic corral, about three hundred feet long. It was shaped in the form of a long oval of sand, mud and grass clumps. Several complicated walkways, towers and observation platforms formed parts of the wall. Evidently the villagers had the craft of clever builders.

Within, several animals, horses and riders milled about. Also of note were stacked bales, targets for archery practice and what appeared to be a track and obstacle course for training purposes.

At the gate, a watchman beckoned the newcomers in. Risgan gave a cheerful smile and Kahel shoved past him with a surly grunt.

A variety of weapons hung from the inner palisade: swords, axes and shields. A dozen young hunters spurred their wild-eyed mounts forth, amid much clamor and gesticulating. In the high-spirited tumult, they whipped lassos over their head to take down young stags, in preparation for live hunts, capturing either young deer or horses for breeding and training purposes. Others drew their bows and fired arrows from their mounts at the targets. Others stood at a hundred paces and aimed at smaller or larger targets depending on their marksmanship. A group to the side wrestled with each other or sparred with mixed weaponry—sword and staff. Risgan's crew stood about, watching with curiosity and amusement, along with several others who had gathered to watch.

A mixture of male and female hunters of both bands, young and old, participated. The clansfolk, it seemed, gave no preference to gender or age.

Kahel sauntered over to examine a trio of young hunters aiming longbows at targets about fifty feet distant. With steely-eyed inspection, he sized up a blond-haired youth wearing red cap and green jerkin who consistently kept missing his target.

"Let me see that bow," Kahel grunted. The boy obliged. "Your bow's of good quality but you're holding it wrong."

"What do you mean?" The boy looked up at him blankly.

"Watch." He raised his brows. "You don't believe me? Try it." He positioned himself behind the boy and placing hands on his, guided his fingers along the smooth curve of the wood. "Grip the middle hard, boy. Yes, like a sword! Squint with your one eye, straight along the shaft as close as you can. No, aim a little higher, yes, that's it, you were shooting too low."

As a team, Kahel and the youth aimed and the bow twanged.

The arrow struck the edge of the target high to the right with the fletch quivering like a peacock's fan before it fell to the ground.

The boy blinked in surprise. "Wow, did I do that?"

"Of course. Your turn. Try it solo."

The boy bit his lip and squinted in deep concentration. His arms trembled, not used to seeing so many eyes on him.

"Wait—aim a little higher," admonished Kahel. "Hold your

breath and stop your quivering. You're like a tail-wagging puppy. That's it. Now shoot!" The boy's arrow caught the edge of the butt closer than the last shot. Certainly far from a bulls-eye, but a significant improvement.

"Wow!" The boy shook his head in sheer amazement. "I've never got that close before."

Kahel winked at him. "Keep practicing."

Arcadia chanced to ride up next to Kahel and flashed him a wry smile. "Quite the bedside manner you have there, Kahel. You could become a good trainer."

Kahel shrugged. "I doubt it. Not my calling. But others have said as much."

On one of the raised platforms rising over the gated section, a group of youths huddled, staring down at the stags running in a penned-off area below. Mygar's brood, judging from their worn brown furs. A few stags were loosed from the side and then caned on the rump to get them running. With grins and mutters the young hunters took aim, fingered their bows and fired blindly with blunt wooden arrows and small, low-powered bows. They seemed to have not much more force than slingshots.

Under the scrutiny of a scowling, cold-eyed teacher, they fired one after another while the instructor barked out brutal criticisms on points of technique and style. "Too slow, Jikrak. The stag's already far out of kill range."

"No! Too fast, and stiff on the draw, Egrek, You're a lousy disgrace. Look, even the stags are laughing at you!"

The youth pouted and hung his head. The sniggers of his friends were demeaning. Wiping his snotty nose, he took aim and fired at a large buck which raised its rack of antlers at him. The animal leapt up with a snort, battering the platform and almost toppled Egrek, then bounded to the end of the corral, only to be pegged by his wooden arrow with blunted end. The beast tucked tail and snorted but was unharmed at that distance.

Kahel grumbled. "Look at them. Easy to take pot shots at a bunch of penned-up animals then laugh and joke about it after. It's as if hunting big game is like bagging birds. It's not the same."

"They have to learn somehow," sighed Risgan.

"I agree though," said Jurna. "I wouldn't do it like that."

The Caerlineans didn't approve of the panicking stags and grumbled loudly at their treatment. The stag was a revered animal, not to be abused. There was little they could do in the wake of Mygar's savage ways and his program of versing the young clan members in live target training. Competition among the young hunters was fierce; improving their skill and speed seemed the priority, all of them eager to join in the hunt and be recognized among the senior hunters of Mygar's band as worthy.

Risgan watched Arcadia trot up on her gray mare. All eyes trained on her.

Horse and rider moved as one, as if she had a secret communion with her steed. Her skill was well known among the clan and something of a point of jealousy among others, including her sister, Thrulia, whom Risgan had taken even more of a shine to. Or perhaps it was the other way around.

On horseback Arcadia could easily outmaneuver the men, having ridden since the age of five. Her long hair rippled across her shoulders with every move of her proud mare.

Risgan had heard whispers that both she and Thrulia had descended from the blood of warriors. It seemed hard to believe, given this defeated and gutless hetman who had sired them. He could only conclude such traits must have come from the mother's side of the family.

After a few swift turns about the track, the riders dismounted and brandished their blades. Arcadia joined the sparring, an excellent swordstress who could best or hold her own against any or all of the others, save Svengar and Mygar.

Competitive sword play was in progress; several youths paired against one another. Ever were the younger contenders eager to challenge Arcadia, for it was considered an honor. The clink of blade on blade echoed across the sand and eyes turned to follow the matches very closely. Arcadia whipped her blade faster than the eye could see. Her blade whirled and she snuck inside her challenger's guard to halt her swordtip before his nose. "Okay, who's next?"

"*Me!*" called out the nearest young man, tipping his woolen cap and clutching his sword with defiance. He swaggered forward, wearing a cocky grin. Arcadia bowed and the youth echoed the courtesy.

They sprang back on the balls of their feet, brandishing their blades. The young man struck first, confident in his attack. Arcadia gave some ground, letting him rush in. She sidestepped and parried his thrusts then snuck in a left and right sequence of her own and in no time she had him backpedaling, tripping over his heels until he blundered and she slipped under his guard and the blade caressed his neck. "Yield?"

"I do," he hissed. His voice, a defeated whisper, was not so soft to escape the ears of the spectators. The others murmured in wonder and cheered.

"And now how about me?" drawled a low voice. Risgan blinked in surprise to see that it was the huntsman Lokbur.

A wide grin spread over Arcadia's face. "You'd like a drubbing, my lord?"

He bowed low. "I'd be honored."

She laughed. Before they could engage, Mygar pushed in and

grabbed Arcadia in a bear hug. He laid his lips on hers so hard that she could barely breathe. It ended in a sloppy kiss and she wrenched herself away finally, gasping, wiping her lips of his slobber. She slugged him hard in the chops.

The others watching laughed and cat-called. Arcadia, quivering in rage, uttered several unladylike remarks. Mygar stood there, laughing uproariously, smoothing out his reddening cheek.

"I love it when you're angry, Cadie. Such a vixen! You and me will go far. I'm in love! Love, do you hear me? Love!"

Svengar, his brawny lieutenant, howled a wolf's laugh. "I believe you are, lord. Such a pleasant sight. It must be spring."

Lokbur mustered a wild leap forth and with a crazed shout, drove in to attack Mygar, sword flailing.

Mygar parried and grunted, striking back with force. "What is it with you, puppy? You want to play? The worse it'll go for you." He lunged in with dangerous speed, slashing several overhead loops. Lokbur was hard put to defend against such furious attack. Yet he parried every stroke blade. Such was his animosity and fierce love for Arcadia that he held his own and it granted him strength and luck. "You're a pig," he taunted. "You don't respect our people." In he rushed, impassioned, angered by the foreign lord's audacity.

But pretty words could only go so far against such a foe. Mygar, not treating the assault seriously, struck again and again with negligent ease, moving in inch by inch with a lion's yawn on his lips.

Ducking Mygar's whipping blade thrusts, Lokbur smacked the giant in the chin, a firm crack across the mouth that had Mygar stepping back and licking his bloody lip with a crinkly grin. "Nice shot, Lok. Wülv's praise. You're getting better. Must be all those oat cakes you're eating in the morning." He laughed, drove in, snorting and grunting with a wild brute strength and smashed the sword out of Lokbur's hands. He kicked him hard in the chest then clouted him with his leathered fist on the side of the head. Lokbur's face grew very purple at the force of the hit. The chief's fist rose and fell, pummeling the younger man until Lokbur's mates jumped in to defend him with savage cries.

The spectators roared. It looked as if full-scale war would take the entire Caerlin clan but then horsemen broke in from both sides broke to separate the two parties.

Risgan, appalled, remained impressed that the whole line of Caerlin members jumped in to defend their clansman.

Mygar gave a rude snarl. "Louts! Idiots! I'll not waste my time fighting stupid cretins like you one by one."

The druid watched from the back of his russet roan with a shrewd cast to his slitted eyes. For a fleeting instant, Risgan saw amusement flash in his face, full of disdain and indifference.

"Seems our young hunter has his hands full," murmured Jurna.

Lokbur staggered out of the knot of figures and slumped down at a nearby table, taking a cup of mead from a barrel. He downed it in a gulp. He looked badly roughed up, his hair matted and blood trickling down his cheek. Risgan came over to check that the young man was okay.

Lokbur's voice came as a hissing rasp. "She makes eyes at me but I have no idea if she even likes me. Maybe she is just playing me for a fool? Maybe I'm clinging to nothing but a boyhood infatuation for her." He seemed to not care about his own wounds, only that he had been disgraced before Arcadia.

"By 'she', I assume you mean Arcadia?" Risgan sighed. "Don't be too hard on yourself, Lokbur."

"Easy to say. Mygar humiliates me at every step. How I'd

like to wring that weasel's neck!"

"So would many."

"What do you suggest?"

Risgan sighed. "Well, easier to wade through that swamp than fathom the complexity of the female race—which is tantamount to saying easier to become a master magician—just ask Moeze." He gave a mocking chuckle.

Lokbur frowned. "Judging from Moeze's skill, I highly doubt I shall."

"Moeze's capabilities are steadily growing," observed Risgan. "Afrid was rather hard on the young buck. He's had a rough handling, so give him some encouragement."

"Did someone mention my name?" A pale face bobbed in— Moeze, a figure in a blue-silver robe.

Lokbur blinked as the magician butted in, eyes gleaming and long, slender fingers clutching a silver disc.

"Need a trick done, a magical incantation written, or curse counteracted? Moeze is your man."

"Not today, Moeze," said Risgan. "Perhaps tomorrow, or next week?"

"As you wish." He bowed with a small curl of lip and glided away.

Lokbur took Risgan aside and spoke in a hushed whisper. "Some practical advice, Risgan, on how to deal with women would be welcome." He rubbed his sore jaw.

Risgan steepled his fingers on his brow. "Lokbur—think of it like this. Women like to be sought after. It makes them feel valued. You've got to give them that feeling of being special, or else they don't feel you care for them."

"Oh, ho, you seem to know a lot about this, Risgan. Sounds good, but can you give me specifics?"

"Use your head!" said Risgan with impatience. He slapped a

palm on the wine barrel. "Get plucky, Lokbur. She's a hetman's daughter! Raise the bar high and higher for Douran's sake."

"You're right, Risgan." He hung his head and ambled off, rubbing his bruised chin.

Risgan frowned, wondering if he'd given the young man a bit of wrong advice. His own success with maidens had been sadly lacking of late.

In all of the four sections of the training grounds—archery, rodeo, horsemanship and sparring—Risgan's companions found a place, as did members of Mygar's and Vardot's clans. Risgan and Arcadia favored the sword, Kahel and Thrulia the archery butt, Hape remained much enthralled with the horse racing, a skill he'd give his eye teeth for.

Moeze was intrigued with the druid and his beguiling jeweled staff, and he approached to trade lore. Dodonis at first fixed stern eyes on Moeze, then gave a slow nod. They went off together, Dodonis's hand on the young magician's shoulder. Meanwhile, Jurna perked up at the talk of several hunters discussing tracking skills in the woods.

"Haven't you heard of setting snares while you scout?" Jurna asked. "That way you can trail-blaze but set certain hunters to pick up the spoils."

Risgan smiled, catching a snatch of the conversation. Jurna and one of the younger huntsman before long became instant friends.

A strident voice intruded on Risgan's train of thought: "Raise your sword, archer! You think you're so fast?"

Risgan turned to raise his eyebrows at Kahel. The archer was practically spitting curses in Svengar's face.

"A deal better than you," Kahel growled. He moved in fast.

"Let's you and me go a round or two then." Svengar's silver broadsword rose in a slithering rasp from his scabbard and caught Kahel's darker blade.

Risgan scrambled over, alarm showing on his face. A sick feeling coursed through his gut. He had a sinking premonition that such a duel may spell the end of them all. He jumped in without a second thought. "I will fight you, Svengar. Raise your weapon!"

Mygar bustled forward. "No," he blurted. A sinister grin spread from ear to ear. "How be you and I go a round, relic hunter? Thus far you've been a big mouthpiece in this village with little action."

Risgan scowled. A hundred eyes watched their movements. To back out now would imply cowardice.

He shrugged and bowed. "As you wish, my lord." He drew his sword.

"My lord! Don't insult me with your fake deference. You mean it as much as my grandmother's dead dog. On your guard, outlander!" He came in slashing at Risgan with a breakneck speed. At the same time Svengar roared and charged Kahel. Their blades met in a mutual, resounding clash.

Risgan barely had time to parry. Sweat poured from his feverish brow and the hair behind his ears as the fur-clad huntsman came charging in, grunting like a hog.

Risgan ducked and rolled. He narrowly avoided decapitation. Mygar was playing for real stakes. He lunged in again and again and Risgan danced about, favoring defense over offense, thinking to play the cat and mouse game where the mouse avoids the cat's paws. This tactic seemed to infuriate his enemy all the more, a game which Risgan relished playing, if not for the fact that one slip could mean his death. But during the dodging and baiting, Mygar slashed the pouch at Risgan's side and all Risgan's magical relics tumbled out on the sand: his pale blue wishbone, and some beads and the lumpy dusk-colored nephrite gleaming a sultry red glow.

Risgan hissed and hastily stooped to cover them up with the black fabric, then he cursed. He rolled aside, barely escaping Mygar's blade. But the baleful, glowering gleam of the nephrite did not escape the huntsman's notice and he paused and uttered a loud oath. "What's this evil witchstone, outlander? Some talisman you're guarding for your magician? Let's have a look at it."

Risgan quickly snatched up the black fabric and stuffed it back behind his belt.

"Nothing to concern yourself about."

"I'll be the judge of that. Let's have it." He laid into Risgan, pushing him back with a series of scythe-like strokes.

It was an unfortunate happening, this sudden exposure of the nephrite, for Risgan had been careful to keep the relics hidden. His teeth ground and with renewed vigor he parried and slashed, catching the huntmaster on the side near the hip, slitting leather.

Mygar, in a fit of rage, spun and crouched low; a boot heel flicked out and caught Risgan in the kidney. Risgan gasped, almost doubling over. Ignoring the pain, he sprang in and as Mygar let down his guard, he leveled his sword tip at the chief's neck.

"You yield now, 'lord'?"

"Yield, my ass!" He scrambled to his full height, swatting the flat of Risgan's blade away. Risgan gritted his teeth, ready to run the blackheart through. But he held his composure, knowing he'd be skewered to death by Mygar's men if he attempted such a bold move. Already the chief's fiercest hunters had gathered round, grumbling in rancor, their blades drawn. Not wishing any further escalation, Risgan held up a hand in a sign of peace. "Let us call a halt to this idiotic roughhousing."

"Fair enough." The Svengali chief grunted in accord. "Enough of these puerile games. We've work to do."

Svengar and Kahel let their blades drop, huffing like stallions, neither of them likewise winning an advantage.

"You stupid striplings!" called the chief at the gawking spectators. "Back to your exercises. We've got hunts to train for." He shook a fist at the youngsters on the platforms and the others aiming at targets. "Kaergli, Minas! Take the outlander to the druid and divest him of his occult talismans."

Someone ran to fetch the hetman.

The druid watched the goings on very closely and gave a crafty nod. Mygar's men joined in lockstep with Caerlin's men to escort Risgan off the grounds. The druid followed along with an eerie relish, rubbing his wrists, a bright gleam in his eye.

Risgan decided he did not like Caerlin's druid.

* * *

Chief Vardot's men accompanied Risgan to the druid's hut, a high, conical dwelling of straw bales and mud. A rank odour assailed Risgan's nostrils upon entering: of earthy herbs, incense, old ash, and something more peculiar. A brazier hung close to the side, a hearth too, unlit and dingy. Old bags and bins of saltpetre lay aside bowls of fat and a long tableful of many talismans and tools: antlers, pincers, stones, gems, clay bowls, herbs and unguents, liquids and pastes.

The hetman, who had joined the party, addressed the outlander with a twitch of nose: "Yes, Risgan, you have been summoned here for two reasons. Barring your useless magician who has exhibited a fledgling and dangerous magic, it is clear that you are somewhat of an occultist, a man harboring magical adjuncts. As you know, spellcraft and magic is strictly forbidden by laymen in the village without my authorization, furthermore controlled by our druids, in this case, Dodonis. Hand over the witchstone."

Risgan swore under his breath. "Impossible, lord. The item in question is quintessentially an heirloom, of great sentimental value."

"Be that as it may, I must insist on the relic." The hetman nodded and signaled to his attendants who unsheathed their swords.

"Very well, lord. If I must."

"Ordinarily I would not care about this, but Mygar is quite adamant about the seizure, and seems to bear some vendetta against you. If he is to be my future son-in-law, I must contrive to keep the peace."

"It is a misguided way of thinking, but understandable, lord." Risgan rubbed his chin. Imbroglios. Too many of them.

Upon relinquishing the piece of nephrite somewhat reluctantly, he licked his lips with discomfort and stared. He unwrapped the black cloth and the talisman fell out on the table, the size of his fist, gleaming a rare glow. His heart pounded. It was a most valuable piece, dangerous if fallen into the wrong hands. He didn't realize how attached he had become to it. Perhaps the magic had infected him more than he cared to admit? The spryness in his step and extra vigor was due to this gem, beyond doubt. He hadn't experienced such freshness of spirit for years! He must get the bauble back. He felt confident that an idea would come to him.

"And this pale bit of bone?" inquired the druid, pointing to the other relic shaped like a fishbone that had spilled out.

"A good luck charm, nothing more. Surely you do not want to confiscate that too?"

The druid waved a hand. "I'll let it go. Anything else?"

Risgan shook his head.

The druid reached for it, but thought better of it. For the

moment he gave it only a cursory inspection.

Wild cheers and drunken shouts drifted from the common grounds, and Risgan imagined Kahel and Jurna indulging in too much swamp-rot grog with the other hunters.

"Oafs," murmured the druid under his breath. "A waste of a life all that ale-guzzling so early in the day. You, I trust, are not of that breed?"

Risgan shrugged. "That depends on the circumstance."

Afrid hissed from her cage of thorn. Risgan stared at her with a contemptuous resignation. She had the face of a young imp and looked ever in fouler mood than before, if such was possible. Risgan instinctively reached for the sealed pouch at his side, noting the cursed nephrite hid there, was there no more.

"A wretched creature," muttered the druid.

"She has committed great sins," agreed Risgan.

"No greater than any of ours," the druid sighed. "Each man or woman thinks his sin is less than the one beside him." Dodonis signaled to his attendant. "Bring in the prisoner." The attendant bowed and left.

"Stay with me a while, Risgan. I wish to show you something."

Dodonis shifted to the table, wise enough, Risgan noted, to use gloves instead of bare hands to handle the nephrite.

A crafty glint entered the druid's eye, as he surveyed Afrid glowering in her cage. "Yes, my little witch. Soon you may yet help me in certain tasks invested upon me by Mygar—this new talisman may help along the way also."

"What tasks are these?" barked the hetman.

"Nothing which you have not already instructed me in. Only to appease his whims."

The hetman glowered with the memory.

Risgan curled his lip in disgust. "You would do well not to

enlist on the witch's help. She's treacherous. Shall I expound on her deeds?"

The druid held up a hand. "That is not necessary."

The servant returned. A giant accompanied him, hauling in a captive whose head was covered in a baggy brown hood. The man, an older slave, Risgan guessed, was thrust forth heavily roped at the wrists and wearing heavy shackles on his ankles from which depended a chain in the hands of his hulking captor. Risgan had never seen a man so large and tall. Risgan stared up at him in awe, evoking the amusement of the druid.

"This is Warscax, our jailer."

The giant gave the chain a proprietary yank. "You asked for this knave, my lord?" The jailer wrinkled his nose at the stench. "You'll want to bathe him soon enough."

"To where he's going, Warscax, he will hardly need it," Dodonis commented dryly.

The prisoner snarled with hate.

"Spit all you want, Moginax. Your fate awaits you. You slit the throat of Verix, our talisman-maker. Remove the hood."

The giant pulled back a flap of the hood to expose a crooked nose and leering mouth.

The grim captive rasped, "Verix was a cheat who frauded my sister and deserved his fate. His magic power tricked her."

"No matter. It is not your call to take another's life."

The prisoner spat a wad of green filth at the druid's feet.

"Very pretty. Recalcitrant to the end. Pity. That is why you must die."

"I care little for your dogma or the laws of this society," said Moginax. "Wülv, your false god, has done nothing for me. Only dress me in filth and with rags and pile me with ignominy. I spit on knaves like you and your hetman who break laws every day, like allowing these filthy raiders in our village."

The hetman bristled. "See to it that he is punished."

The druid had no answer and looked away with a glassy stare. Risgan felt awe and pity for the condemned, who looked one step closer to death.

Dodonis ripped back the hood more now to reveal a surly face with red welts, pocks and scars. Dodonis gripped the nephrite with a thick leather glove and shifted it toward the prisoner, raking it across his pocked cheek and bare arm.

The prisoner stiffened, opened his mouth for brief instants they gurgled several incomprehensible words. He hawked another wad of filth, jumped and jerked about spasmodically, yanking at his chains. His gray hair stood on end then became a shiny brown color and his skin looked much younger and his eyes blazed and gleamed with vitality.

The druid stepped back with wonder. "The magic of youth and age. So, the sorcery is real!" He turned to Risgan with a new look of appraisal and twisted the gem in his palm to expose its lighter side. He raked it cruelly across the prisoner's other cheek. Moginax loosed a howl of anguish and stiffened and his hair seemed to grow to a lighter shade of gray.

The druid gave a sharp inhalation. Rubbing his chin, he frowned at the glimmering relic, whose mystical dusky-red glower could inspire the imagination, especially of the ambitious. "So, I must keep this object in my possession for further study."

"Have it as you want, Dodonis," said the hetman. "I'm weary of spellcraft and have no head for this magic. See to it that Risgan meets me in my chamber after you are done with him."

The druid nodded. "Very well, lord."

The hetman turned on his heel. Dodonis had few more words to share with Risgan and ordered Warscax to thrust him into a back cubicle, little more than a closet. Risgan, waiting at the door, gnashed his teeth in fury, trapped as he was in the dark. He heard many grunts and howls and pleas. A flapping and scuffling, as of vials and pots tumbling off the table. He winced. Some time later, the door jerked open and the druid stood akimbo, lips parted, hair askew and his chest heaving. The hooded figure lay slumped in a heap and Risgan feared he had killed him with his liberal application of the nephrite's magic. "I have no further need of you," the druid said. He gave a brisk flourish and signaled to the jailer. "The magic is alive and well. Take him back to Vardot."

The Caerlin guards escorted Risgan to the hetman's longhouse near the communal hall. A break had been called from the early training session, for several of Mygar's men loitered about the communal grounds, plopping apples in their mouths from the dinner barrels or ogling the Caerlinean women. Risgan waited in impatience before the hetman's door. The sound of angry voices ensued, slipping from under the cracks.

"Mygar comes from a powerful line of warriors," said the hetman. "His family lineage is on the Herstag side of the wolf. I have promised you to him."

"It is ridiculous," came Arcadia's voice.

"I have promised you to him...to keep safe the clan and peace in our land."

"Then you're a bigger jackass than I assumed. They make a mockery of our customs, Father, camp next to us with their boors and motley clot of wild animals, and even harry us, goading us on their hunts. Do you think they'll stop at me, Father? He'll demand more and more of you—until you have nothing left."

"Perhaps, but I know of no other way at the moment. You

do need to marry."

"It's Lokbur I love," she cried.

"Lokbur?" the hetman snapped. "Forget him. He has good intentions but can do nothing against Mygar's mettle. You saw what happened to him today."

"Why don't you fight him? Are you that cowardly?"

"And be cut to ribbons? Is common sense stupidity? He has too many wild men. He watches us like hawks. We aren't what we used to be, Arcadia."

"Then let us train, Father. We'll trick him, ambush him."

The hetman's weary grunt came back as a muted hiss. "We've been through this before, Arcadia. I admire your spunk, I really do, you have the fighting quality of your ancestors in your blood, particularly your mother's. But it's not enough. We can't win this war." He sighed. "It's a shame Malcina passed so suddenly."

"Better to die fighting than to be a kept animal," she muttered. There came the sound of breaking pottery and the door jerked ajar. Arcadia stormed out, almost bowling over Risgan. She pushed past him, angry tears in her eyes. The golden arrow rattled in her quiver. "Out of my way, you outlander."

"Milady—" said Risgan.

"Go! I don't want to see anybody now, or listen to any more dogma."

After the outburst, the hetman ambled out with a weary step, running his fingers through his hair, damp with sweat. He was in no mood to see Risgan or any others and flourished a quivering hand. "Go back to the training ground. I'll see you in the evening." He closed the door.

With a shrug, Risgan hastened from the hall after Arcadia. He caught up with her, out of breath. "Milady, wait."

"You," she huffed. "I told you to go away. You can do nothing for me."

"Are you sure?"

"I'm sure."

"Milady, If I can help you in any capacity, I will."

"What can you do?" she wailed. Her face was a tear-streaked mess. Her hands thrust in her vest and fixed on a charm in the shape of small unicorn figurine which she worked in her palm. "I pray to you, mother Driadis," she said, "that you will send these wretched invaders far away. That you will guide me on my path and tell me what I should do." She closed her eyes and murmured several prayers in a tongue Risgan had never heard.

At that moment, Risgan saw a strange light in the sky at the fringe of the forest. The form of a unicorn, he guessed, the head at least, but with the body of a woman. He blinked to ensure he wasn't hallucinating. She floated up into the boughs and stood on a branch clutching a golden arrow. He blinked again and rubbed his eyes. "There!" he cried. "Look! Arcadia, a sign." And yet, when he looked again the image was gone and the huntress was striding away.

Risgan wet his lips and cast her a solemn gaze. An urge of whimsy came over him that he could not fully explain. "I have the wishbone," he blurted. "I am not without means. I will employ the magical might of this talisman to make things right between you and Lokbur." He pulled it out, pale blue shimmered, and yet, it looked an almost ordinary thing. "It is the only thing your father and his druid didn't confiscate from my person."

She stared at the talisman with curiosity. "What is it? Is it better than my unicorn charm? It seems not to work any more and I grow doubtful of Driadis's power."

A brief flare of memory surged in Risgan. He recalled the

unfortunate predicament leading to his exile. The Pontific's wrath. The heat of the Lady Farella who had been at the heart of it all and who had left an impression on his heart, which he could not rid himself of.

"I acquired it at the market in Zanzuria some weeks ago. The rest I'd rather not say. They are sensitive issues."

She shrugged and turned toward the enemy camp.

"Where are you going?"

"To face down Mygar."

Risgan blinked and ran to get Jurna. The journeyman loitered by the communal well, waving his sword and trading angry words with one of Mygar's hunters.

The two caught up with Arcadia and together approached the wolf chief's hut where among others he lived with his wild band in the makeshift camp. The place was a shambles, dogs roaming around sniffing piles of garbage, some smoking heaps. Stray fires burned and crackled, over which huddled figures roasted river eel. A band of crude huts lined the river bordering on swamp; hunters milled about with their women, ragged-haired and unkempt, hints of rough song and rude talk lurking about the periphery.

A stag head was nailed to Mygar's door, the carcass given to his stray dogs to devour. Risgan curled his lip. Arcadia's mouth hung loose as the dog's muzzles tore at the meat and the naked ribs of the carcass with growls in their throats. "You butchered that stag for your own sport."

"And what of it?" said Mygar. "The dumb beasts are here for sacrifice."

"The gods will curse you," she spat.

"Not my gods," Mygar laughed. He thrust out a long arm and snatched the golden arrow hanging in her quiver. "From now on, I'll be the guardian of the magic arrow."

She gasped, reaching for it. "You can't."

He slapped her hand away. "I just did."

"It's sacrilege. The arrow is the symbol of our people."

"Not any more. I'll use it to slay these pesky isks that invade our skies. So far you've been incompetent and haven't managed to thwart the leader of the flock." He tossed the golden arrow to Svengar who came ambling up, and they both laughed.

"Take it to Dodonis," Mygar instructed. Have him ensorcell it with richer magics. By eventide of my wedding, we'll have cleared the skies of every isk from here to Bazuur!"

Arcadia turned away in disgust. She marched off, fuming while Jurna cast the chief and his crony a chilly glare and Risgan hurried after her.

Risgan caught up with Arcadia and made efforts to speak but she jerked back in anger. "That louse has stolen the symbol of our ancient power. It will demoralize the clansmembers and weaken us even more."

Risgan gritted his teeth. "I will get it back for you."

She blinked at him with amusement. "Are you some miracle worker, relic hunter? First my love life you promise to repair then you pledge you'll return me my clan's magic talisman? Pah! What can you do?"

"You'd be surprised," Risgan said dryly.

* * *

Later that day, Risgan ducked back behind the shadows of the blacksmith's home and unwrapped the wishbone from its black cloth. He rubbed it until it was warm in his palm just as the peddler who had sold it to him had instructed him. He closed his eyes. With all his strength he wished that Arcadia might have her dreams realized. It was a longshot. Whether the magic was potent enough to fulfill such a request, Risgan did not know. He only knew that if it worked, it could save this village from disaster. He also knew it only worked if the bearer believed in the magic. He had seen it work in the hands of the Pontific's young son in the market of Zanzuria. A miracle had happened. He snickered, recalling the horrified shrieks of the courtiers as they crouched bare-assed in the market.

That evening when the blacksmith Kevil had retired, Risgan gathered close to his companions around the hearth and spoke in low whispers. "We must retrieve the golden arrow—for Arcadia and her clan."

"What, are you crazy?" Kahel griped. "Why should we risk sticking our neck out for these people? They hold us here against our will and would slay us if either of the two warring chiefs demand it. I don't know why we are not contemplating an escape right now."

Jurna looked at Risgan. "He has a point. We could probably sneak past their scouts this very minute."

"Except we'd have to collect my relics...which are in the druid's hut now along with the arrow, and we still have Afrid to deal with."

"Sod Afrid!" sneered Kahel.

Risgan ignored Kahel's outburst. "I have ulterior motives in my thinking, Kahel. I'm thinking three moves ahead. The golden arrow is a weapon that we can use against Mygar. He's our real enemy. Steal it and we have leverage against him—then we can escape. If we try to sneak out of here, they will come after us with their horses and men and cut us down. Without it, it will be a tough road with many risks. We can kill two birds with one stone, and get my relics back."

Kahel turned away with a growl. "Count me out."

"Fair enough. Hape?"

"Me? Why me?" He looked around blankly, seeing their expectant looks.

"They will not suspect you, plus you are good at creeping around in the dark."

"What? And you aren't?" Hape was clearly not pleased with the arrangement.

"Moeze," breathed Risgan, "this time you and your wonky spells can come in handy. Pay Dodonis a little visit and draw him out. Get him off balance while Hape grabs the golden arrow." He smoothed his hands.

Kahel shook his head in disgust and walked away.

"Moeze? Are you in?"

The magician gave a silent nod.

"Good, then I will work as overseer. Jurna, you are backup. Stay here and hold the fort. Run interference if things go sour." Risgan took him aside. "Convince Kahel to help you, if you can."

Jurna grunted with a grin. "Right."

Hape sighed and made motions to creep out in the dark.

"Hape, wait—" Risgan grabbed his shoulder "—don't forget my piece of nephrite. I must have it back!"

Hape gave a crisp nod.

Jurna looked at Risgan in bewilderment. "Are you obsessed with that thing? Something unhealthy about that relic. It has a dusky look to it."

Risgan pursed his lips; his youthful hands clenched. "Let's just say, Jurna, it is more important than you think." He forbore telling him about its sinister youth-and-age magic and the hold it had on his own. There was no way to communicate such things without raising alarm.

* * *

The night was wholly dark, black as the burnt pot, and the moon, a waxing crescent, lay obscured behind ragged clouds. The communal fires had burned low and voices drifted as mere murmurs, ghosts of the night, with straggles of drunken men returning from their revelries to their lodging to recoup for another day of hunts and training.

Crouching low, Risgan crept on stealthy feet. Moeze and Hape loped after him across the common grounds past the bridge to the other side of the village where the druid's hut resided. A golden glow spilled from the open window. The druid was still up, hard at work. Risgan gave a short sigh. Perfect. He grinned. Ducking between a pile of firewood and two squared-off compost bins, he motioned the others forward. Moeze clutched his silver disc in a pale hand. He rapped on the door and Risgan ducked back deeper in the shadows.

The druid answered. "Who is it? Oh, you? What do you want?"

Moeze bowed. "Moeze the magician, at your service, Dodonis. Pleasant to see you. I hope the evening is treating you well—"

The druid held up a hand. "This is no time for a house call, Moeze. Be gone, I am busy." He moved to shut the door.

Moeze stuck a foot in the door. "Wait! My associate Hape the Homeless and I, have come to discuss business—

"What business?"

"Magic, what else?"

The druid sneered at that and cast the intruders dire looks. "I haven't time to waste on tyros. Why are you two skulking like spiders in the dark? I have an important task entrusted me by Mygar—which will have no end, and this cursed witch of yours, is not cooperating."

"You don't say? You mean, Afrid? I can help you with that."

"How?—You know her spells?"

"By heart. All of them."

The druid scowled and looked left and right. He worked his

lips then beckoned. "Come in."

Risgan covered his mouth in a snicker of triumph. Hape and Moeze doddered in.

Risgan risked a peek through the window. The golden arrow sat on the table amid pots of steaming liquids and unguents, glowing a golden red. The druid had been dipping its diamond tip in some mixtures, but seemed entirely dissatisfied with the results, judging from his flushed scowl and his animated gestures. From what Risgan could grasp of the ensuing conversation between him and Moeze, it seemed that Mygar had entrusted the druid to infuse the arrow with an extended magic so that he could kill all the isks in one go and gain ultimate power over all the clans. A lofty goal. Risgan curled his lip. Dodonis was just arrogant enough to think he could pull it off.

Moeze gestured and laughed with carefree ease, showing a face of cheeky confidence. Lifting his disc, he rubbed the magical shimmering side.

The druid's face darkened in a scowl. "Put that away, Moeze. What are you crazy—"

He had no time to finish. An explosion racked the confines, blowing up in everyone's face.

The three of them went flying. Hape banged against the wall. The hut dipped, sagged and seemed to press outwards, as if the most foul wind blew through it, tousling the druid's sandy-colored hair, and rifling the straw bales and pitching him backwards. Moeze was thrown sideways.

Risgan gasped in horror as he saw the smoking hole in Afrid's cage. She staggered out, eyes agleam with fierce triumph.

Risgan gave a sharp intake of breath. Here she was, crawling across the mud-packed floor. He was about to burst in, but stopped. Let Moeze and Hape handle it. The plan would either sink or swim on its own two feet. He heard Afrid's hissing and blubbering like a baby in an attempt to mouth spells to lay waste her enemies in the hut.

"Contain that witch!" bellowed Dodonis. "Idiot!" He groped about in the smoke. The sounds of shouts and the pounding of feet of villagers grew. "What were you thinking, magician? My precious sanctuary—my herbs, staves, ruined!"

Moeze bit his lip. He coughed and lifted his blackened disc in the direction of Afrid. To no avail. The magic was spent.

Afrid stumbled out of the hut whose door now hung on its hinges. While the druid's attention was diverted, the magician's fingers grabbed at a black-wrapped object that had tumbled to the floor.

The village grounds swarmed with figures. Hands tried to snatch at Afrid. She slipped through their fingers like a greased pig. She fled off into the night. All was an indistinct blur; figures rushing hither and yon and Risgan skulking by the pile of firewood and the waste barrels of compost. He laughed when he heard the screeching oath of the druid and a similar howl of an enemy huntsman victim of Afrid's teeth.

Moeze and Hape tottered out of the hut, blundering into Risgan, soot-blackened and scratched. Risgan steered them away from the hut. Moeze and Hape were out of breath, their eyes gleaming in the dim light from the dying fire. Other torchlight brands bobbed nearer.

Risgan seized the arrow from Hape's nerveless grip. "Good work, Hape!"

"A messy night's work,' Moeze professed.

"And the other item?"

Moeze shoved the black fabric in his palms.

"Good lad!" Risgan's lips curled in exultation. "That nephrite means more than you can think." He tucked the package under his belt. "Quick! Let us bury this arrow while the hubbub is about. Back to the blacksmith's! When our druid finds the arrow gone, there will be hell to pay."

They bumped past several panicked villagers eager to discover the source of the explosion. "Hurry!" Risgan hissed.

He turned to address the villagers in an overloud voice, "There's been a fire and a terrible accident! Fetch buckets of water from the swamp. You there, young stalwarts—form a brigade!"

While the village youths filed in confusion to obey, Risgan motioned Hape and Moeze on, then trailed after with a sly grin.

Jurna was waiting in the shadows, crouched by the door. Kahel was inside snoring. "Took you long enough," said Jurna. "Well?"

"The good news or the bad news?"

Jurna rolled his eyes. "The good news, Risgan, please start with the good."

While Risgan hastily buried the arrow in the shadows back of the longhouse, Hape told Jurna in a few words what had transpired at the druid's hut.

Jurna went suddenly tense and looked left and right. "So Afrid's escaped?"

"Vanished."

Jurna sucked in a wild breath. "That's bad news."

"She—"

Risgan put a finger to his lip. "Quiet. We've not time to waste on Afrid now. Quick, inside."

* * *

A rigorous search of the fugitives yielded nothing in the morning. The obvious suspects had been ruled out—Moeze and Hape. No magic items could be found on their persons. Vardot and Mygar stood around arguing, glaring daggers at one other.

Risgan took Arcadia aside to whisper in her ear that he had buried the arrow behind the longhome and described the place exactly where she could find it.

She blinked in surprise. "Relic hunter, maybe you are a miracle worker after all…"

Risgan tipped his head. "At your service. The least I can do, milady."

Afrid was still at large and nobody knew where she was.

Kahel stood about in slack-jawed wonder, his throat thick with a derisive snort. "How far can a baby-faced midget get?"

The question sat heavily on the members of Risgan's company. They knew only too well the witch's capabilities.

After a time Mygar gathered his hunters and brandished his sword. "Move out!" he bawled. "We can't be worried about some dumb witch and a missing arrow. The hunt goes on! Be ready in a half hour."

* * *

The day dragged on. Gray skies stretched from horizon to horizon, east to west, investing the twitchwoods of Fandar forest with an eerie silence. Majestic trunks ranged to either side with thick ropy bark, trees too old to fathom, trees beyond the clutch of time. Boughs creaked to the movement of vagrant winds.

Risgan and his band were not outfitted with mounts as he had earlier hoped. Instead Mygar and a dozen of his grubby, fur-cloaked rogues forced them to scout on foot with many huntsman's bows trained at their backs as horseman kept them under constant watch. Risgan, Jurna and Kahel were prodded along as the main band rode behind them with bows trained ahead. Kahel alone had his bow to scout ahead and flush out animals while Jurna kept his hunting gear and sword for tracking, and Risgan his knife, sword and club. If Kahel tried to shoot at the horsemen, he would be quickly arrowed down. So, Risgan and Jurna made no attempt to escape.

Moeze and Hape had stayed back at the village. Moeze was still detained under suspicion of colluding to steal the arrow, Hape deemed totally incompetent at such thievery.

Kahel's dark scowl bore testament to his disgust with the whole thrall of indenture and his wish to be free of this damp, woody place. "This land and its endless salt marshes and midges has none of the charms of my eastern hill country," he complained.

"Perhaps you shouldn't have wandered so far afield then," posed Jurna.

"And what of your own falling afoul of Afrid? It doesn't count? Speaking of which, I hope that hag has wandered far and will cause no mischief?"

Risgan held up a hand. "I have no doubt she's up to more shenanigans. Dodonis will have a fine time catching her."

"You think so? I don't trust that hedgehog farther than I can throw a paper bag. Conniver's got his fingers in every pie in the oven."

"Shut up, you weasels," growled Svengar. "There's hunting to be done, not gibbering. You're scaring the animals."

"What animals?" croaked one of the huntsmen. "There's not a gopher in sight in ten miles."

Jurna knelt and felt the soft earth. Certain patches showed the outline of the hooves of stags. "Look, stags roam these lands. These prints are fresh, not an hour old."

Mygar jumped off his horse to examine the tracks. "So it is, tracker." He cast Jurna a look of new respect.

Risgan waved a fist. "Onward then. Let us catch these four legs and be done with it."

Mygar looked at him with amusement. "We'll go when I say we go, outlander. Don't give my men orders." He gave his men a curt nod. "Onward, Svengar."

Risgan shook his head with a bitter laugh. Oaf. He mumbled under his breath, then traded meaningful looks with Jurna.

The next two hours passed with fruitless return. No stags, no unicorns. Not even a measly hare. Perhaps the animals shunned Mygar's stink and and the land on which they trod? Risgan couldn't quite comprehend it. Likely it was the isk attacks of the other day that had spread a taint over the lands.

Ever were the hunters' eyes turned to the sky, dreading the swoop of another renegade isk. None came, perhaps daunted by the loss of their unlucky brethren not three days ago. Arcadia had gone off on her own again, much to the vexation of Mygar. "Where is that wench?"

Svengar shrugged.

Kahel grumbled. "This is useless. The stags are too aloof and canny today. Let's all spread out to flush them out."

"No, we go as a group," muttered Mygar. "I don't trust you rabble to beetle off in the bush—or scare the animals off."

Kahel shook his head. "At least, let us fire-flush the stags out then."

"What are you talking about?"

"What, you've never heard of fire-flushing?"

The horsemen flashed the archer blank looks.

"You know, set some bonfires at strategic places—spook the stags? Get them running out of their places of hiding, so then your hunters can take them down."

"Sounds like a worthwhile plan," one dusty horseman grunted. He rubbed his chin. "It might work."

"Of course it'll work," scoffed Kahel. "Just make sure you don't burn the woods down. Otherwise you'll have no stags to hunt."

Mygar took a breath with an effort of patience. "That goes without saying! You think we're a bunch of idiots here? We'll try out your idea, but not today."

"Why not?"

"Because I said so." He gave his head a mulish shake. "Might burn the forest down."

Kahel just shrugged. "You'd be surprised. I've seen it done before."

Mygar rolled his rangy shoulders. "I said, we'll try it out one of these days. Keep your eyes trained ahead."

Upon Kahel's continued glare and no sight of game, he sighed. "Okay." He signaled Svengar with a brisk chop of hand. "Go! Escort these outlanders. Light some fires, or whatever tricks he speaks of." He squinted at the sky. "With rain coming, I don't see how effective anything involving fire's going to be."

A grim smile broke out over Kahel's cracked lips. Risgan grinned.

* * *

The fires were set and the hunters drew back into the thickets, waiting with drawn breath as smoke drifted to their nostrils. Motion came from the nearby woods. Kahel beckoned them down.

Two stags came bolting through the underbrush. "There!" he cried. One of Mygar's men's arrows caught the fleeting shape high in the midriff. Svengar's arrow nailed the second.

The horsemen reined in on Mygar's signal and circled the fallen prey. They looked on in triumph.

"Chock that up for our count, Mygar." Risgan said with triumph.

"I might," said Mygar. "But I'm thinking that these two stags are largely a product of my men's efforts, not yours, building fires and whatnot."

Kahel lanced him a silent glare while Risgan and Jurna rumbled oaths from the depths of their throats.

Arcadia happened to gallop in on her gray mare. Her heart sank when she saw the slaughtered animals, especially as it triggered the inevitable memory of the head tacked to Mygar's door. She had lost all desire to kill animals. Her quiver was still full of arrows and her hair held a garland of twitch sprigs and a may flower.

Mygar roared in displeasure. "What have you been up to, little flower? Collecting herbs?"

That got some laughs out of his men.

"None of your business," she said.

Risgan allowed himself a grin as he cast her a thoughtful glance. Her left hand dug into her jerkin pocket. Probably fingering that unicorn amulet of hers. He didn't doubt she had been praying to Driadis more often than not. He knew the feeling, praying to gods, magical powers. His own hand strayed to his wishbone many a time and not without some success. The magic was real, though he hadn't a clue how it worked.

Ever since the attack on the unicorn, Risgan noted how Arcadia had been less keen on killing animals. Specifically, she had refused to take part in target practice in the last two days as if she had lost all appetite for blood, unlike the other enthusiastic hunters.

Only two stags had fallen to their credit. A poor showing if Risgan ever saw one. Stomping out the fires, they all made their way back to the village, practically empty-handed.

Tempers had flared upon the low yield of the day and a palpable tension settled over the group. Jurna accidentally trod on Kahel's heels and Kahel rounded on him in anger. "Careful there, journeyman." Kahel wrinkled his nose. "You reek of burnt ash."

"What, and you don't?" said Jurna.

"Quiet down back there," called Mygar. "A day's a day. Sometimes the hunt yields few fruits."

One of the hunters muttered, "We'd have got none without Kahel's innovation."

Mygar hissed and gave his head a sour shake. Risgan thought it was a sullen acknowledgment of the truth.

Tired, exhausted, scratched by brambles, the companions examined each other and their soot-grimed faces with weary scowls. Their ragged leathers clung to their skin, soaked in mud from plunging through creeks and marshland.

Risgan, dissatisfied at the turn of events of the day, frowned. At this rate it would take weeks before they could wipe clean their indenture. He planned on getting away from Caerlin before then and its breed of roughnecks. But maybe not too soon with luck like this. He fingered his wishbone and discarded the idea of using it. An overused magic was a weak one.

A fugitive form, a wispy white tail and a white and black body, eased out of the brush. He could not be sure, but he guessed it must have been the unicorn. Why was it following them? Didn't it sense the danger? He opened his mouth to alert the others but closed it once again. What was the use? These brutes would slay the creature without a moment's thought. It was bad enough to have to kill stags, let alone majestic animals such as these. At least the villagers, unlike these barbaric hunters, used the meat and hides for sustenance and clothing, whereas Mygar and his bullies would nail their antlered heads to doors and hunt them for sport.

* * *

The wedding was fast approaching and much preparation was in order: a grand feast and celebration that included dancing, drinking, various entertainment, acrobats and a new village play, whose subject matter still remained a mystery. The call for extra stags and drink was on and hunters scoured the woods searching for any game possible. Vardot could expect extended peace with the alliance of the factions so he was particularly pleased. Arcadia was not pleased and she sat with Thrulia by the fire, downcast and wringing her wrists. Risgan a put in an encouraging comment as did Jurna.

Moeze told stories around the fire of the old magicians of Romaric. A topic that aroused some small emotion, but even this did not cheer Arcadia or others like her sister. Risgan was about to ask Thrulia for a dance, but he thought better of it. Better to let her console her sister. Kahel approached with an armful of sprig and threw it on the fire, sending it crackling and hissing. A tart smoke wafted in Risgan's direction.

Arcadia waved a hand to ward off the stinging cloud herself. She leaned into Risgan, brushing his arm. "It seems your magical wishes have availed one thing at least," she murmured, forbearing to mention the arrow.

Risgan leaned over to whisper in her ear. "The item is safely hidden?"

She nodded.

Risgan loosed a breath. Thank Douran, she had recovered the arrow. He hoped it would take down many isks. "Do not give up on the other matter, milady. Miracles are known to happen."

She shrugged. "They'd better happen quickly, Risgan. The wedding is in five days. It will have to be a rather large miracle."

He turned to see the enemy chief stumbling over on heavy feet. He plopped himself down at Arcadia's side, wrapping an arm around her shoulder with an oily leer. "Arcadia," he jeered, slurring his speech. "So good to see you. Why so dour? Not becoming of a pretty maid to shed tears. Aren't you happy? Your nuptials should be a source of joy."

Arcadia shirked away as if the rank-smelling chief were the bearer of some plague. Svengar moved in to take a seat at Thrulia's side. He was wearing his usual foxish grin.

Risgan stiffened. His hand instinctively reached for the handle of his club. But he hesitated, recalling what had happened to the last horseman who had crossed Mygar.

Lokbur spoke in a frost-laden voice, "Don't you have other business to attend to, chief, like stripping hides or gutting eels?"

"Go back to your cave, Lokky boy. Your place is back there in the outhouse." Svengar laughed along with other hunters of Mygar's band who had gathered. The chief leaned in to place his lips on Arcadia's ear in an oily kiss. "Come, Arcadia, my dear. Let us repair to a more private surroundings so we can test each other's mettle before our nuptials." He laughed, an ale-ridden laugh, gross and reeking, as he placed a meaty mitt on her shoulder.

She drew back, looked him up and down in contempt. Jerking to her feet, she pulled loose of his weaselly grip. "Frankly, my lord, I'd rather bed down with the goats out in yon yard."

Mygar's face went red despite his drunken mood and his teeth rattled in his mouth. He snatched at her wrist and painfully pulled her back down beside him.

Risgan lurched to his feet and Lokbur was at his heels. Risgan reared in and smelled the grog on the huntsman's breath. "You're drunk, Mygar. Go back to your quarters rather than regret doing something foolish in the morning."

Mygar gave a raspy chuckle. "Oh, is that right? Get away from me, you puppy." He slapped Risgan back and shoved Lokbur aside.

Risgan drew his club. "I'll not stand by and see a maid's honor sullied by a conceited boor."

"You won't will you?"

A dozen figures appeared out of the shadows—all Caerlin men bearing swords and bows.

"Very touching," said Mygar. "Get out of my way, relic hunter, or you'll regret it." He drew his knife in one hand and his sword in the other. "The wench's mine. Her father's promised me, and she'll learn respect, by Wülv!"

Svengar stepped in, his eyes darting over the grim gathering. "Come, my lord. Not the time for a squabble in our drunken states." He grabbed the chief by the arm.

"Hands off, you mangy dog."

Svengar swore. "Let it go, Mygar, none of us are in the mood for drunken rows tonight. Tomorrow we'll spill blood, and plenty of it."

"Piss on tomorrow!" Mygar spat. He imitated Svengar's whiny voice, "Blood I'll spill any time, Svengar, anywhere. You're a damned sissy." He swept off his nephew's arm and hefted his blade. "I'll go when I damn well feel it. Or do you want to play chief now?"

Svengar's shoulders drooped. Yet Risgan could see the rage etched in the scarred face and his fingers clenching on his sword with the urge to smack sense into his drunken uncle.

Moeze twitched his nose and held his silver disc close. In the blink of an eye, Mygar's face became suddenly very furry and rosy as if he had sprouted a new beard. The chief scratched his cheeks like a hound with fleas and began to bay like a dog.

Arcadia began to laugh. "My lord, I didn't know you were auditioning for the comedy hour at our wedding."

This earned chuckles among the Caerlineans as Svengar dragged the cursing, scratching Mygar away.

Risgan shook his head and patted Moeze on the back. "Good riddance, Moeze. Always a new surprise with you."

The magician smiled. "Sometimes spells can come in handy, can't they?"

"They surely can,"

Risgan's cheer was shortlived. He dreaded the wrath of the chief in the morning when he was sober.

CHRIS TURNER

3: The Last Hunt

The final hunt of the season was on and Risgan and his men were only seven stags away from fulfilling their indenture. All five trudged ahead through the green and silver trees, clutching bows, swords or knives while Svengar and eleven of his mounted hunters took up the rear. Moeze and Hape accompanied Risgan and the others this time, dragging their heels and grumbling. Risgan had appealed to Vardot, stressing the need to work as a team, without which they were losing out on capturing stags. It was stretch of truth, but they had a better chance in numbers at escape and Risgan had a plan.

No freshly-slain stags slumped over Svengar's or the other huntsmen's mounts. Mygar, mercifully, was absent. Only his right hand man rode with the group, the brute Svengar with the scar down his left cheek, and bared muscles with tattoos despite the chill air. The plan was to meet up with Mygar's team later that afternoon.

"Pick up your feet," Svengar growled, "we've got many miles to cover and the stags aren't going to catch themselves."

Risgan kept walking without a backward glance. His throat was parched and his belly groaned with hunger from lack of proper breakfast. All of them woke up a little too late to get full fare and somewhere lady luck had failed to give them leftovers. Somewhere there had to be some good news in all this. In the huntsmen's eyes, Risgan saw only resentment, that they couldn't ride free and full out to catch the stags.

Moeze sighed. "Even my cursory magic is failing to flush

out these crafty stags." He gave a weary frown. "Why is it that every time I try to help out you people someone always grabs my shoulder and cautions me, or says, 'hey, Moeze, please relax and don't strain yourself?'"

Risgan spoke in a casual tone. "Your magic is too profound, Moeze. A master mage is not to be enlisted in such plebeian applications as this. Even that trick with the beard last evening was beneath you. You should be saving kingdoms and rescuing princesses from fierce dragons!"

Moeze straightened his back. "Yes, right, Risgan! How could I forget, and I'm glad somebody recognizes the fact."

Jurna tried hard not to cough.

Arcadia came pounding out of the brush on her gray mount after some mysterious venture.

Svengar turned and swore at her as she came reining in. "Woman, you should be back with the others! There's no solo excursions allowed. You heard Mygar, unless you wish to directly confront your future lord."

"I wish to confront no one. Unless it's only a stupid policy—I'll ride free where I wish." She fixed him a glare. "Besides, it's dull riding with you and others—my 'betrothed', for example, is a dreadful bore. All he talks about is halters and arrows and bows and swords and how much fresh meat they're going to take and how much ale he can gorge at the next campfire feast. I'd rather go off on my own. I urge you to show some respect. Being a chieftain's bride can have its perks—or can rebound on you should you displease me."

He laughed at that. "You're Mygar's whore, nothing more. Or soon will be. You'll have no status once you're under his heel."

She grimaced at the prospect. Risgan took pity on the maid. If it were him, he'd run away before marrying that lowlife,

Mygar.

Ominous black dots roved high in the skies well out of range.

"Isks," groused Kahel. "There can be no doubt what's on their mind."

"Aye, scavengers," hissed Svengar. "What else is new? Why do they wait?"

"They fear our arrows, lord." One of his henchman lifted his sword. "When we are most vulnerable, they will strike."

"I know that, dolt. I just didn't give them the benefit of that much intelligence." He grunted. "Curse the thief who took the magic arrow. Now we have no surefire protection against the beasts. If they swoop all at once, we're doomed. One of us will likely die. I'd skewer the whole lot of those miserable predators with that arrow."

"Pretty boast there, Svengar," said Risgan. "Can you back it up though?"

"Quell your tongue. Let's get this hunt over. A sour feeling brews in my stomach. I like not the taste of it."

"Nor I being downwind of you," muttered Kahel. One of Mygar's hunters laughed.

The hunters spurred on their mounts, forcing Risgan and his band to lope along at a faster pace. Before long they were huffing and puffing like whipped cattle. Arcadia looked on with heartfelt sympathy. "Give them some slack!"

Svengar gave his head a stubborn shake. "Mygar told me to work them hard after last night's escapades. What is that extra quiver you carry on your back, lady?" He tipped his head in an insolent way. "Surely you don't plan on bagging a hundred stags today?" He laughed.

She examined him with cold grace. "Perhaps I will, Svengar."

One of the black-toothed men next to him hissed. "Svengar, there." He pointed—it was the same unicorn from the glade on the first day. Its slick white pelt was smeared with old blood from the isk attack. A magnificent creature, with its sleek flanks brimming with health and a golden corn proud and true on its head and wild, blazing blue eyes. The crafty beast stopped just short of bowshot as if it were goading them. Risgan gazed at it with an air of uncertainty.

All eyes turned to the slender shape poised at the edge of the woods. They were downwind of the unicorn so it hadn't detected them yet.

"That animal'll land us a pretty prize," said Svengar, "its hide and head nailed to Mygar's door."

The hunters grumbled their agreement.

Svengar gave a cruel leer and lifted bow and took aim, but Arcadia spurred her horse to intercept, a shriek on her lips. She knocked his bow arm, fouling his aim. The unicorn skipped away to the copse ahead unharmed.

"Foolish witch!" he cried as his arrow slammed harmlessly against an exposed rock.

Wheeling his horse around, he tucked bow in his saddle and snatched at his sword. "You'll pay for that insolence. How dare you?" He charged after her but she spurred her gray mare on through the woods and bolted for the open ground after the unicorn. "Ride, Spinifex, ride!" She laughed at Svengar's feeble attempts to catch her. Her mastery of a horse far outweighed his.

Svengar gnashed his teeth. "Don't just stand there, you fools! After her! I want the wench caught!"

The horsemen reined in their mounts and crashed through the underbrush. Kahel took opportunity to charge into the thickets in the opposite direction. A grunt of satisfaction rumbled on his thick lips. Risgan and Jurna took to their heels on diagonal paths with Hape and Moeze splitting between the two.

"Get them!" Svengar roared. He spurred his horse and kicked out at the huntsman's beast next to him. "Nastra, after those ragbags."

"Haha, lost your wards, have you?" crowed Arcadia back at him. "Mygar's going to skin you alive." She brandished her blade as she galloped on. "Won't be just me he beats silly," she yelled. "Which is it going to be, Svengar, the outlanders, or the unicorn?"

Risgan continued to crash through the underbrush, Jurna not far behind. The sound of whinnies and men's curses echoed on their heels. What to do? So many variables. Risgan's brain spun.

He dodged around the tree trunks, scratched by many brambles and thorn. Leaves slapped at his face. Gradually the shouts and the horse hooves faded away and he began to hope that maybe they'd win free.

Round up the others. A voice spoke to him. There was safety in numbers.

"Moeze." He hissed at a moving shape deep in the thickets. "Quiet down." He gathered the shivering magician to his side.

"An arrow missed me by an inch," Moeze quavered.

"Don't worry, you're alive. Where's Hape?"

"Back there." He pointed to the dark tangle of trees.

Risgan winced. He tugged the youth along. If only Hape didn't wander too far. There was a hunched brown-robed shape shouldering his way through the trees. They hurried toward him. He was unharmed, a fierce and pale look of triumph on his face though at his new found freedom.

Kahel and Jurna stalked out between two ancient massive

twitch oaks, whose roots clung to the leaf-covered soil. They wielded their swords and bow. Jurna had no difficulty tracking Risgan and the others.

"Good, we're all here." Kahel patted Risgan on the shoulder. "For once, I'm happy to see you, relic hunter. Let's make as much of this as we can. Starting with as much distance as we can get between Svengar and his goons."

"What of Arcadia?" asked Risgan.

"What of her?"

"We should hunt for her. They'll harm her."

Jurna barked out a laugh. "They'll never catch that wild one—nor us, if we're crafty."

So they wandered through the mysterious elder woods until Arcadia's fierce mare broke out of the underbrush. Her face was flushed and a glow of triumph burned in her cheeks. She had doubled back and managed to outflank Svengar and his men.

She drew beside them. "Quick! Follow me, if you wish to be free of those rogues. They'll be coming for you and they're not far away."

Risgan broke out in a wild grin. He scrambled after Arcadia with the others on his heels. He gestured to Hape. "Come on, Hape! Move your butt."

"I'm coming, Risgan—as fast as I can."

Arcadia plowed ahead through the thickets, over brooks, fallen logs, hills, dells, brackish pools, hollows, across untouched glades, through forests older than time, ever stranger and more enchanted, always far ahead of them, and she seemed to be following something.

At last, they came to a glade deep in the forest. Risgan estimated they'd wandered for an hour or more. Only it was not a glade. Risgan peeled back a screen of vines to peer on a vast ruin of shattered pillars and a great dome-shaped building in the middle. A temple appeared somewhere out of time: a hundred feet high, four hundred feet long. Riddled with spires and crusted gems. But the stone walls were blackened with age and infested with ivy. Shrubs grew from the cracked courtyard leading up to its main entrance where a black gap spoke of a ruined portal.

The huntress drew them no farther and she sat atop her mount, staring in mystified silence. Out of breath, Risgan turned back to gaze upon her. "How did you find us?"

"The unicorn," she said in a breathless voice. "I followed it here. Why I don't know."

Risgan choked out a startled cry. "The unicorn? How?"

"None of us will know." She lifted a trembling hand. "There, that's the temple of Driadis." Her voice faded to a whisper.

"How do you know?"

"The legends speak of it. Lost. A fable." She blinked, her eyes full of wonder. A small tear glistened down her cheek. "None of our clan has ever seen it. The unicorn led us here. Our twistings and turnings so far from our hunting grounds must have led us here."

"Where is this unicorn?" said Kahel. "I've not seen hide nor hair of the animal since Svengar chased us."

The weather had begun to shift. A cold wind blew and with it, a freak rainstorm. Hail came thundering down from the gray skies, pounding on their heads, driving them to shelter under the trees.

Unusual for this time of year and the ragged company grumbled.

The sound of hooves clattered on shattered rock. "Down!" hissed Risgan.

Arcadia checked her horse and she scrambled to duck beside

them. She clicked her tongue; dutifully her horse backed behind the thickets out of sight. They crawled behind a rubble of stone, some ruined outbuilding where a cover of twisted branches blocked the force of the rain and hail. The temple lurked a few hundred feet away.

The forms of three mounted riders rose from the rain mist and ice pellets.

"Of all the wretched luck," Risgan muttered. They'd tracked the unicorn or followed the huntress. Or perhaps she'd followed them here.

"I seem to have underestimated that louse Svengar's tracking skills," mumbled Arcadia, ducking lower in the dead leaves.

The horsemen drew nearer. The echo of voices sounded over the patter of rain. "Curse this falling ice," one railed. "The black wolf Wülv speaks. The gods are angry with us, Svengar. Angry."

"To Douran's tits with your fear and superstition, you fools. There's no 'wrath' of the gods. You've been duped by those pious druids. What gibberish has that priest Dodonis been feeding you?"

"They fled this way," growled the third horsemen. On Svengar's signal, they moved out of earshot.

Arcadia peered out upon the ruined courtyard and lifted a hand. "That unicorn," she hissed.

Risgan risked a glance and saw the graceful creature poised at the black gap leading to the massive domed temple. It sniffed the entrance, one hoof raised, then turned about, flashed them a queer glance before venturing into the dark gap. Why did it do that?

Arcadia's jaw dropped and she rose to gather her mount.

"Where are you going?" Risgan hissed at her.

"To draw the hunters away."

"Why? Wait here."

"No. Remember, I have a mount, and you don't."

She cut him off, hopped on her horse, and clicking her tongue, urged Spinifex out in the rain, a short canter in the ruined courtyard.

Risgan shook his head. He saw the horseman clacking closer. "Stupid girl. She'll get herself killed."

"If she wants to sacrifice herself—"

Risgan waved Kahel to silence.

The voices drew nearer.

"They came along this side path. There's somebody lurking about," grunted one of Svengar's horsemen.

"I can see that, monkey-brains. Their mud prints are plain, but there's a jumble of them that disappear in various directions. But they seem to lead to—Look! Well, I'll be a flying monkey. That vixen bitch huntress. After her!"

Risgan squinted through the screen of vine-covered trees and caught in the daze of the moment, he watched Arcadia clatter over on Spinifex and disappear into the ruined temple. Svengar and three of his horsemen whipped their horses hard and Risgan groaned in dismay. They waited tensely, expecting her to come out of the side, but saw no movement. All was dead still, everything too uncannily quiet here in the lonely wilds.

Risgan swore. "A trap. She's trapped! I know it. We can't let her fight them alone, Jurna. Svengar's in a murderous rage. He'll kill her. You saw, she lost him his prize, the unicorn."

"He's right," murmured Jurna.

The freak hail storm had changed to drizzle. They clambered after her, like weasels, through the wind and rain, across the courtyard of stones and weeds poking up through the cracks, the witch shrub with wild purple flowers. Kahel shook his head, wondering aloud at the folly of women.

Jurna ducked inside the jagged black gap, then Risgan. Hape clambered in next. Moeze gripped his silver disc and Kahel shouldered him aside, moving into the half darkness like a thief in the night.

A thin, watery light streamed down from broken casements, notched squares cut in the stone. Even in the dimness, Risgan perceived the presence of spirits here beyond the ken of human understanding. The place was overgrown with weeds and choke vine. Tendrils had broken through the floor and curled up the walls.

They wormed their way forward on their bellies, hardly daring to breathe.

Crumbled pillars ranged around them, forming something of crude circle. Elsewhere the stubs of three rows of ruined inner pillars rose. In between the tallest foremost, a cracked statue of a unicorn stood rearing on its hind legs. The effigy was awe-inspiring, if not scary. An altar, some low slab of marble propped up on carved unicorns' legs, rose out of the splintered stone like a monolithic ghost of the past.

This cavernous space was huge and littered with broken masonry of sublime and eerie design, half-broken statues of leaning pillars. At one time the place had been beautiful, a work of art, with magnificent paintings on the walls and designs carved in the domed ceiling, but these had all cracked or disintegrated, or lost the battle to vines over the ages. A pool of water lay in the centre, investing the air with a musty smell. The rustle of rats bristled in the gloomy distance.

Risgan stared on high, trying to make sense of the dim shadows. Giant statues of unicorns and half unicorns with human bodies lined the upper galleys. A stair had once given access to the tiny, vine-shadowed windows on high, but it had long disappeared, crumbled to ruin and lay toppled in stony desolation. No way of getting up to those windows to pluck the gems that to a relic hunter's eye would be worth a rare fortune.

An agonized snorting alerted him. In the near distance they discovered new horror: Arcadia's horse, Spinifex lay sprawled in an pitiful heap. Evidently the mare had slipped on the shattered tone and broken its hind leg.

Where was Arcadia? The animal, still wheezing and struggling, would have to be put down.

Shouts and the clack of steel echoed from within. *The huntsmen.*

"Come!" Risgan snarled at the others. They picked themselves up from their bellies and raced after.

There before the altar four figures loomed.

Risgan held up a hand and crept closer, urging his comrades to stealth.

Svengar brandished the golden arrow, plainly wrested from Arcadia, and his two henchmen pinned her against the wall. She looked lost and defeated, her hair tousled and a bright red welt across her cheek where she'd been struck. Her arrow was snatched again, at the mercy of these ruffians, and her horse lay mortally wounded.

"Let's have some sport with the woman before she's wed to our 'lord'." A mean-eyed lout gazed at her, licking his lips. "She looks a tender morsel. No one'll know, and I'll make sure she doesn't talk, won't I, mistress?"

"Get away from me, you pig!"

A faint smile tugged at the corners of Svengar's lips but he scowled. "It's a pleasant thought, Burkit, but I'm not in the mood for such rompings, especially in these dank precincts. Such an unpleasant environment. God, I hate these holy places, especially moldering ones. Though I'd like to see her punished and humiliated, if not cowed for losing me that unicorn. Strip her!" he ordered.

"With pleasure, lord." The mean-eyed man leered and ripped at her jerkin and bared a breast while the other held her.

Svengar sneered. "Where's your unicorn god now, lady?"

"How about here?" Risgan looked down at them cheerfully from the altar. He'd crept up behind it and crawled up the back. "I'd wisely suggest you unhand the woman, Svengar, and step back slowly, unless you wish my bully-boy archer here to lay you full of wood."

Kahel stepped out of the shadows with his bow and Jurna at his side, broadsword brandished. Hape and Moeze were next to appear, Moeze's silver disc whirling.

The hunters growled and froze. Arcadia twisted in her leather and covered herself up.

Svengar whirled about. "You? Outlander. I have bones to pick with your mangy hide." He nodded to his henchman. They did nothing to obey and he growled a gross insult to let Arcadia loose. She stumbled past Svengar and lurched, reaching for the arrow, but he pulled it back at the last second and leered at her. She spat in his face.

She came running toward Risgan, on the verge of tears. Risgan grabbed her and held her in his arms. "There, are you hurt, milady? Moeze, see to her!"

Risgan signaled to the journeyman. "Jurna. Divest these cretins of their weapons."

He gave a cheerful nod.

"Milady, you are hurt."

The huntress clutched her left arm and shoulder. "'Tis nothing, Risgan. Those brutes, I thought they were going to—to—"

Another echo clanked from down the hall. Horsemen by the clatter of their hooves. The members of Risgan's company crouched, tensed.

Svengar grinned. "Well, relic hunter. Your move. It seems matters move to a new condition. What will you do?"

Risgan thought fast, his eyes darting right and left. Even as they did, some horrendous sliding of stone came to his ears, like fingernails dragging across an endless chalkboard. A massive stone fell, creating a booming echo, blocking the entrance and much of the light with it, plunging them in deeper gloom. Dust billowed and men shrieked.

Svengar and his men bolted. Bedlam broke out in the half gloom.

Risgan hissed. There was no mistaking that hulking form, walking his black mount. *Mygar.* Two shadows and more followed him. Horsemen. Others crept behind him at his heels.

But the crashing boom? Mygar or one of his henchmen must have triggered an ancient snare. Risgan and his allies grimaced and crept for shelter. Now they were all trapped in this preternatural temple of some ancient goddess.

Risgan rallied the others with silent gestures and he ducked behind a rubble of a fallen pillar with Moeze and Jurna at his side, checking his breathing, daring not breathe. He didn't know where the others were, he just hoped they would stay quiet and keep out of sight.

He heard Svengar hissing to Mygar in the gloom. "So you found us."

"Not hard to track your blundering trail."

"You know of this place?"

"I'd think some foul crypt or temple to their pansy-faced god. How do I know?" Mygar's eye roved to the arrow Svengar clutched in his hand. "Where did you get that?"

"Arcadia had it on her."

"Arcadia?" Mygar blinked. "What do you mean?"

"She was here, and is still lurking about somewhere. I tore it from her grasp before—"

"Before what?"

Svengar licked his lips. He looked away.

"Damn you, you stupid oaf. You let her escape?" Mygar leaned over and smacked Svengar hard on the mouth.

Svengar whipped his head back, wiping the blood from his lip. "You're getting good at those pot shots, Mygar. Even for one who struts around like some lumbering animal who can't even control a few weakling clansmen."

"Careful there, Sven. You're treading on thin ground."

"And so what if I am? Those ragbags stole the arrow from right under your nose. I got it back. Now they are laughing at you."

"Where are they?" the chief snarled.

Svengar flung up a hand. "Here somewhere with the girl. The same grubby thieves who you let live. Mr. Big hunter and chief."

Mygar's eyes kindled with wrath. "Svengar, you're an ungrateful cur. I gave you everything! That title. That horse, loyal men and command, and what do you do, you mock me?"

Svengar's face twisted in confusion, perhaps regretting his words, but the ball had rolled down a slippery slope and there was no stopping it now.

Yet Mygar was distracted and his eyes rolled with greed at the sight under the vine-covered stone. Serpentine was embedded in the altar, a deep jade hue. Such was worth a fortune in the open markets of the cities.

"Burn this place!" bellowed Mygar. "Loot the altar, carve out those emeralds. I want them now!"

"But lord," spoke one of his men, "the jewels have lain here for an age. No one has taken them. Perhaps they are cursed."

"Shut up!" Mygar swatted him away. "Take them and be gone. Driadis be damned. We'll ride to Caerlin and burn that bloody pigsty to the ground. Stupid traitors."

A sinuous shape suddenly rose from behind the vine-covered altar, glowing a pale luminous blue. A slender figure rose from the gloom in a swirl of misty gray cloud, wearing the head or headdress of a unicorn, but having the body of a woman, nude to the waist.

"What sorcery is this?" cried Mygar in a brassy tone. The horses bolted, spooked by the apparition.

Svengar laughed. "So, Mygar, are you going lame on us? It's the druid's work, this ghostly spook. Or that incompetent magician's."

"Moeze?"

"None other. Last time he was skulking about the druid's hut accused of being accomplice of the thievery of the arrow— Now he's here. Though how that nitwit conjured this up is beyond me."

"His magic can still kill." Mygar stared fearfully at the hovering apparition.

"He couldn't burn himself out of a paper bag. Him or his puerile pyrotechnics."

Svengar's eyes bulged white and he clutched his throat and bent over double. His two men recoiled, grimacing. The goddess rose, or rather the unicorn who was the goddess rose, a luminous avatar that cast cold unicorn eyes upon the villains before her.

Mygar sneered. "Out of a paper bag, eh, Svengar? You silly fool! There's magic here at work. Look at it. And you've insulted the gods."

Svengar wrenched himself out of the invisible grip clutching his throat. He choked on his tongue, gasping for air. "Wizardry!" he croaked. He clawed for his sword. "Search this place. Flush out the magician." His head turned. A sudden motion came in the dark. "Ah, there he is. Lop off his head."

Risgan gave a warrior's cry and surged in, smiting Mygar's men. Moeze was on his heels, his silver disc shimmering.

"A barrel of mead to the man who gives me that magician's head," cried Svengar, "served in fresh blood!"

Risgan's club thudded against the fur-cloaked hides of his enemies. Jurna was at his other side. Kahel drew the string on his trusty bow and plugged arrows into the fray while Arcadia faced off against Mygar's closest hunter.

"Ah, my little flower," called Mygar. "You are here. I was beginning to think Svengar a trifle mad."

Arrows flew at them but Moeze's spinning disc cast a warp on the air and caught the arrows in its glowing swath. Risgan's heart stopped as one curved aside, aimed for his chest. While the men stood stunned, Hape ran up behind them and conked them on the head with rocks.

The battle raged; men died and cried out as blood splattered the crumbled altar of Driadis and ran thicker still. And still the goddess floated on high like a nimbus of wonder, as if reluctant to intercede in the petty squabbles of foolish mortals.

Svengar gained control of his senses and fired the arrow; it missed Risgan's head by a hair—the relic hunter could still feel the wind of it—as it ricocheted off the gray stone behind him and smashed some hanging stone projection. It must have struck some lever, for a strange grinding sound echoed in the hall. The floor underneath the fighting figures jerked sideways; everyone was knocked off their feet.

True to its enchanted form, the magic arrow came sweeping

back along its rainbow arc and began its descent back to the bearer. Svengar lay nose first on the cold, moving stone, his face a ghastly grimace as the worst was yet to come. The arrow's light illuminated the ancient hall in multi-colored clarity. All saw the floor slide back, as if by magic.

Risgan teetered on his heels, swaying, catching at the last minute the edge of floor, as the stone opened up underneath him. Hape and Moeze jumped to safety, grabbed an arm each and hauled Risgan up. He lay there gasping beside Arcadia and the others. Mygar and his henchmen plunged down in the pit with the wails and groans of Svengar and the last survivor in his ear. Two had cracked their skulls on impact.

The survivors gasped as one of the horses fell too, breaking a leg on the floor of a great rectangular pit, fifteen feet deep of sheer sides. They untangled themselves from a knot of arms and legs and blinked; Svengar crouched, shaking his head, snatching at the magic bow that lay at his side and fitting an arrow in its strings.

"What is it?" demanded Jurna in puzzlement.

"I don't know. Some pit. Arcadia?"

"Never seen anything like it," she murmured.

Risgan cautiously peered over, only to see the glint of the magic arrow of Svengar's aimed his way. He pulled his head back. The arrow shot up and whizzed by his ear to smack somewhere else up on the ceiling. Risgan swore. It came arching back into the pit, its diamond tip unscathed.

"That thing's dangerous."

"Rotten losers," Jurna grumbled.

"Let's kill them all." Kahel gripped his bow and drew near the edge of the pit in a bent-kneed crouch to peg off Svengar.

"Wait! I'm sick of killing," cried Arcadia. "We've done enough killing." She stepped in front of Kahel, blocking his shot. "It's a miracle any of us are still alive. Only the fruits of the goddess's work. I've been praying to her. Perhaps that's what this is all about. Maybe this is what she's planned for them."

"What about the arrow?" snapped Jurna. "It's down there with those scum."

Arcadia pinched her lip. As much as any, she was reluctant to let the arrow go. It seemed that a war of wills passed within her.

Jurna gestured. "I tell you what you do, huntress, let them starve down there. Come back in a month or two and get your arrow. Then they'll just be a bag of bones."

She wrinkled her nose at that. "It's a gruesome idea."

A curse came from below, as of acknowledgment of the idea.

Risgan looked down and ducked at the sight of Svengar pointing the arrow up at him. He rubbed his chin, racking his brain for a solution to the problem.

"They deserve nothing more than to suffer a cruel fate," rumbled Kahel.

Mygar shook his fist up at them. "We can pick you off all day!"

Risgan shrugged. "It's your call, mistress."

She bit her lip. "They'll stay here. I'll send for some horsemen at a later time, if I feel pity in my heart."

"If we can get out of here," Moeze pointed out.

Kahel shook his head. "I still say we should kill them." He crept over to the edge, dipping back with a growl. "We have the high ground. I can peg Svengar off from up high."

Risgan pulled him back. "No. Arcadia's decided."

"You're a fool, Risgan."

"Well, I've lived this long."

"One day too many, I think."

Mygar clashed his sword against the wall. "Shut up you imbeciles and listen. Help us out and I'll show mercy. If not my men will come and kill you all—even you, milady, for my patience is not inexhaustible."

Risgan looked down at him coldly. "Let them cool their heels in that crypt. Might teach them some lessons in cruelty."

Mygar bellowed, "You'll pay, you filthy outlander. I'm going to tear you limb from limb with my bare hands, even if I have to rip every stone from this damn dungeon." He leapt, purchasing for handholds, but only slipped back.

Jurna gave his head a sad shake. Moeze studied the three prisoners with a philosopher's curiosity, as if wondering how such an intricate predicament could have been orchestrated. Risgan pondered no less the intricacies of fate.

They made their way to the entrance, only to find it blocked, as Risgan guessed, by a massive slab of stone jammed tight to the edges with no chance of moving it or squeezing around the sides. It was in the shape of a unicorn goddess, fallen headfirst from on high. The horn had pierced into the flagstones, effectively pinning it in place.

Risgan looked left and right. "Where is the unicorn?"

The men stared at each other dully. "We've not seen it."

"But you saw it come in earlier, did you not, luring Arcadia into this dank place?"

No one had an answer. Arcadia just looked away with a puzzled frown.

They passed the wounded mare, snorting and thrashing on the cold stone and Arcadia knelt to console Spinifex until she could bear it no longer. On a heart-choked nod to Jurna, she looked away as Jurna ran it through, putting it out of its misery. The young huntress clasped hands to mouth and wept.

* * *

A solemn mood fell over the companions. Hating to see the huntress cry, Risgan inclined his head in the direction of the back of the temple. "Spread out," he whispered. "Hape, you take Moeze down that way and see if you can find an alternate exit. I'll console her." He turned back to the others. "Jurna, Arcadia, let's go this way."

He put a hand gently on her shoulder and guided her away from her dead horse. "Milady."

She wiped away a tear and snuffled, brightening as she pulled back the vines that covered the broken pillars and stared entranced at the rows of script carved there. "Look, there's more writings on these walls."

Risgan frowned.

Shattered tablets lay in a pile at the foot of a small shrine flanked with marble unicorns on their hind legs.

"This is the craft of the old gods," Arcadia murmured. "Driadis and Argonos whom we used to worship until the warrior druids came and infected our tribe and forced us to worship their gods."

Rows of animals were inscribed on the ancient walls, at one time dyed with pigments of various colors: unicorn, deer, fox, bear, wolf, raven, stags—all in communion with the goddess in the wilds.

"That old script conveys the lore of the animals—the unicorn, wise and compassionate, the bear strong and true, the wolf sly and mysterious. All are sacred to the forest and play their part in the overall scheme. To kill them, especially the unicorn, is a sacrilege."

"What of wolf furs and the leather that you wear?" jibed Kahel.

"Maybe the wolves should shear men of their hides for use

104

as rugs for their cave dens, I think."

"It's an interesting concept," mused Risgan.

"Look…on these tablets are written the teachings of Driadis the Great."

"How do you know?" grunted Jurna.

"I studied the scripts. My mother was adept before she died. She imparted me the gift."

"What does it say?" Jurna asked.

"It says, 'Seek virtue in kind hearts. Forgive the wounds your enemies have inflicted on you, though they will never be your allies.'"

"Right," Kahel snorted, "like anyone's going to forgive that scum Mygar and his gang. Does it say we should maybe give the brutes a charity hug for all the woe they've caused you and your clan?"

"Enough, Kahel," said Risgan.

Arcadia laughed. "You have a way with words, Kahel. I'll give you that."

Risgan paced back and forth, seeing no solution to their dilemma. His pacing brought him past the endless rows of figures and script and closer to the altar and his fingers instinctively reached for the wish bone in his pouch. He closed his eyes, rubbed the pale bluish bone and wished for a miracle.

"Staring at a miserable altar isn't going to help us, relic hunter," muttered Kahel behind his back.

Risgan nodded and turned with grim resolve, forcing a tight smile, almost tripping over the thick vine that crawled across the floor. "More of Mygar's horsemen may be lurking about the shadows and it won't take them long to find us."

"They can't get in though, can they?" Jurna pointed out.

"If they do—"

At that instant the altar trembled and a pale blue form rose again, its luminous glow lighting the ancient stone. A slender woman garbed in leathers of the hunt rose this time, but with the same headdress of a unicorn.

They stepped back with croaked murmurs in their throats.

"Goddess!" Arcadia gasped. She immediately dropped to a knee and bowed her head.

The luminous figure nodded and lifted a pale hand. "Child, do not flee, there is nowhere to run." Risgan blinked and stopped dead in his tracks.

The head turned to gaze upon Kahel and Jurna who had raised bow and sword at her shimmering form. Slowly the weapons hung slack in their nerveless hands. Moeze approached and stood pinched-lipped. Hape was at his side, his mouth hanging speechless. Risgan sniffed and licked his lips, his mind in a turmoil, a flurry of thoughts racing down shadowy corridors.

The disembodied voice spoke, "The huntress and the outlaws have finally teamed up. I'm glad of that."

"Wh-what do you want?" Arcadia asked.

"I want nothing. It is more, what do you want?"

" I—I really don't know."

"Isks haunt the skies and you don't know? The power of Driadis wanes in these dark days, and you have no desire?"

"Goddess, I—"

"No need to backpedal, Arcadia. The isk is the dark minion of Wülv, you know it, child—an instrument of terror, rapine and bloodshed, and the embodiment of cruelty. Spawned in the underworld itself, through the devotion of ignorant worshipers who don't know what they pray for. The unicorn, the splendid avatar of Driadis, is ever pure, protector and healer that watches over the forest and its innocent denizens. Anyone who reveres the unicorn is brought luck and prosperity. So it is taught by the priestesses of the old ways. Those who go the way of the isk and worship death are rewarded with blood and pain—like those wild huntsmen who languish in the pit, the ones you fear and the ones whom you fight."

Arcadia stammered. "But—"

"You abandoned your old gods, the Driadis whom your mother showed you at age six. That is why your sacred arrow has been snatched from you and even now lies in the clutches of your enemies."

"But, I had the arrow," she protested.

"By whose grace did you have it?"

Risgan recalled the strange light in the trees back in Mygar's camp and what had prompted him to win back the talisman. He stifled the rasp in his throat that grew to an ache of sadness.

A tear raced down Arcadia's cheek. "I didn't abandon you, goddess, I swear. I say a prayer to you every morning!"

"And that is why I protect you, child. Never fear, the others who worship false gods will fall prey to isks and worse. Close your eyes and dream. All of you!" She gave a gentle command, soft but firm.

Risgan felt his head droop. After a short time and a sharp breath later, he dreamed he was in a lake, swimming with a raven-haired beauty of such enchanting presence as to make his breath catch. She dove with ease into the clear water; he followed her with strength and speed, kicking and diving deep, and they visited many fabulous underwater realms: kingdoms of coral and seaweed and stone. A million years seemed to pass in the blink of an eye. Risgan yearned to kiss the fabulous maid and learn her secrets and she turned about with brazen energy, a challenging smile, a fluid heat, and their lips met for an instant, only an instant, then he was whisked back to the present, this strange, fey hall of the goddess, and her unicorn statues, left still feeling wet and damp with seaweed on his skin and the sultry press of the maiden's warm lips on his.

He wiped his mouth and licked his lips, yearning for that moment when he could still feel the sweet damp taste of her.

The presence of the floating goddess was so peaceful that he wished he could dwell here forever. But that was impossible, and he was snatched back at the sound of a familiar voice.

"What in Douran's name?" Moeze snapped out of his trance, blinking in astonishment. "What was that all about? I recalled being in a horse-driven carriage. My father had given me a strange toy—a wondrous, fabulous unicorn! All white and gleaming of polished porcelain. A magical thing, some curio from yesteryear. It captivated me and I grew up wanting to be a magician. How crazy is that?" He shook his head, as if not knowing what was reality or fantasy. "I've heard it said that sprites can ensorcel a man's mind in the forest, but…"

The goddess smiled at Moeze's evident bafflement. "Yes, Moeze, they can. What would you like it to be—real or imaginary?"

For once, Moeze was at a loss for words. His silver disc sagged in his hand.

Hape murmured, "And I was in a bower aside a pool of water amid the trees of my childhood, surrounded by great animals of the forest—bears, wolves, tigers and lions."

He shook his head in wonder. "Parts of it didn't make sense, but then a weird feeling came over me as if I awoke from a poignant dream."

"We all experienced some wonder," admitted Jurna.

Yes, all of them had been whisked off to some place or time in their past, thought Risgan.

Kahel grumbled, "Nothing but sorcery. Tricks of the mind," he refuted. "This unicorn woman before us isn't real. Just an apparition." He turned to Arcadia. "Say it, huntress, what fiends of imagination did the magic pull up for you?" But Arcadia would not talk. She only wore a puzzled expression, as did Jurna. Both were so moved by the experience that they looked away from each other and would not share their experiences.

"Goddess, you confuse me," Arcadia began. "I hew isks, and even hew men and spill their blood yet you ask me to be a 'protector'? It makes no sense to me." She clutched at her brow. "My head reels with the discord of it all."

The goddess shimmered and showed a kindly face. The unicorn horn on her brow shimmered and her eyes were bright. "It is not an easy thing to grasp, child—the cycle of life and death in this strange, violent world is ever complex. Even the greatest philosophers have come to no reasonable conclusions. They shake their fists at the gods and curse fate. But it is not fate—it is destiny. Only this can I say: while you are hunter and warrior, you must fight the moral fight and kill when the need arises. While you are protector, you must protect the weak and just causes, as your heart guides you to."

Her form began to fade.

"Riddles and maxims," grumbled Kahel. "What are we but just playthings to the gods?"

Arcadia wailed and beat her fist on the altar. "Wait, goddess, wait, how can we escape this place?"

"In my home you are always free, child. *Follow the light and the secret way out will reveal itself to you.*" She shimmered and faded and no more.

Kahel jeered. "Don't make it too easy for us, goddess."

Risgan sighed.

"One thing for sure," intoned Arcadia, "I will protect the ones worth protecting more than ten times the amount I kill!" Her voice echoed with the thunder of defiance.

Risgan nodded his approval. "'Tis a good plan, milady."

Jurna consoled her with a rough pat on the shoulder. "If it means anything, huntress, I think that's what the goddess was trying to tell us."

"But what does she mean, the secret way will reveal itself?" muttered Moeze.

"Don't look at me," Jurna hissed. "Maybe time to put some of your fancy pyrotechnics to work here?"

"Oh ho." Moeze lifted his nose in the air. "When you're in a bind, you solicit my expertise. Forget it, Jurna. Every other time you've rebuffed my services as if they're a plague of ages."

"That's all in fun," the journeyman persisted. "No time to get uppity, Moeze. One of your firecrackers will do, just bust a hole in—"

But Moeze had already stalked away.

"Magicians!" Jurna threw his hands up in exasperation.

"Forget him," Risgan bawled. "We need to find another means." He pulled Jurna and Hape aside and whispered in their ears. "Hape, you're a rat, good at quarrying and burrowing and finding hidey holes and secret exits and tucking in for places of the night. Find us a way out of here."

"Right."

"Jurna, you help him. I'll take on Moeze and Arcadia and try to talk some sense into our magician."

"Follow the light…follow the light," came Moeze's echoing voice as he mused. "What could that possibly mean?" He tapped finger to lip.

Hape caught up with him and tapped his shoulder, "Well, the only light is coming from those windows."

"True, true, and what of it, Hape?" Moeze bit his fingernails. "How to get up there? The staircase to the upper gallery is crumbled, you can see it as well as I, and it's a good thirty feet up."

Risgan huffed. "Hey, I thought we were going to split up and try working in groups?"

They ignored him. Kahel grunted and shook his head. "Even if we could get up there, Moeze, how would we get down? We'd break our ankles jumping that distance down to the courtyard."

Arcadia gave a despondent sigh. She plumped down in the molder, her head in her hands. The others looked left and right in despair. It seemed hopeless.

Hape rubbed his chin, finger to his lip. He gazed from the wall to the rubble then to the vines that crawled everywhere, then back to the window, his eyes glinting in a sudden inspiration. "What if we could use this vine somehow. Loop it around to make a—"

Arcadia and Hape's eyes met. "A rope. Of course. Are you thinking what I'm thinking?"

"Good one, Hape!" Jurna clapped both of them on the back. "We make an excellent team. We'll fashion a rope of the strongest cords. Why didn't I think of that? Kahel, if we can tie enough of those vines together to hold our weights, then we could pull ourselves up."

"We'd have to hook it up there somehow." Kahel's eyes, narrow slits, grew to pinpoints in the dim light. "Possible. Just possible, journeyman. If we could snag it on that projecting beam up there…"

Risgan mused. "Or you could try that unicorn's horn."

"Easy," Jurna affirmed. "We could create a grapple of sorts with some of these fallen blocks."

Risgan and Kahel withdrew their knives and began hacking at the stoutest vine crawling on the walls and floor. Jurna and Arcadia twined them together.

"We need a rock as ballast, to tie the end to," asserted Jurna. "Before long they had thirty five feet of vine gathered in a coiled heap. Kahel took the end and tied it around a suitable block, knotting it tight.

Like a sailor whipping a ship's anchor, he whirled it at his waist and tossed it on high. The rock smacked into the crumbled ledge above and sent broken bits of stone raining on their heads.

"Ow, you clod," groaned Moeze. They fled, holding hands over their heads.

"Careful, already!" hissed Risgan. "This place is already a walking booby trap."

Kahel grumbled and tried again. His second attempt yielded better results.

With a grunt of satisfaction, he tossed the grapple and yanked it back at the appropriate moment to get it looping around the unicorn's horn. No easy feat. He gave it a firm tug and grinned in approval. "Not bad, if I say so myself. "Holds my weight. Any takers?

Risgan looked to Arcadia. "Milady?"

"My pleasure."

She gripped the vine and began the ascent, grunting with the effort. The vine swayed; eyes looked up and Risgan held it taut. At last she crouched on the narrow ledge, breathless and waving down at them. Jurna was next. He grunted his way up; then came Hape, Kahel, Risgan and Moeze who was afraid of heights.

The magician swayed on the ledge, wiping his brow. "Agh. Don't feel too good, Risgan. Never been a fan of heights."

"Well, don't look down."

Kahel shook his head, mooning his eyes.

Risgan risked a glance and saw the trapped huntsmen down

in the pit glowering with rage at the fugitives making their escape. They shouted curses up at Risgan and his band. Risgan and the others patently ignored them.

Risgan pulled the vine rope up and fed it through the nearby window from where cool air drifted in. He couldn't help but notice the gargoyle-like realism of the nearby unicorn whose stone horn had saved their skins, half leaning over the edge of the ledge. The work of a master craftsman. This one sported wings and yearned to fly over the forsaken temple and its time-eaten grandeur like an angel. After double-checking the line was snug, one by one, they climbed down, hand over hand, to the dark puddles of the court below. Risgan paved the way, the first to stand on solid ground. He held the vine and called notes of encouragement to the others.

The sky was gray and the drizzle had abated but a chill wind still blew through the courtyard, rattling the bushes and tousling their hair.

Arcadia shivered and wrapped her arms about her waist. "As much as I adore Driadis, I'm glad to be out of her house and back in the fresh air again."

"Not so lucky our chums back there," said Risgan, jerking a thumb to the looming dome that towered above.

"My heart bleeds," said Kahel.

"Let's get as much distance as we can from here. Arcadia, we need to see you back with your father."

Arcadia's eyes lit with gratitude. They loped off at a respectable pace, their boots crunching on the shattered flagstones. They left the ancient temple far behind…though Arcadia's mood was as gray as the sky at the loss of her good steed Spinifex.

* * *

"My aching head," groaned Svengar. "Who in the seven

hells built this pit?"

"How should I know?" Mygar scratched his brow and wiped away the blood that trickled down his scalp. "I should club you for triggering that trap."

"Me? It was you." Svengar rounded on him and each looked on with daggers of contempt, fists clenched, ready to bash in each other's skulls. They crept about, exploring the wall with their fingers, ignoring the third man of their party, one of Mygar's troop. No handholds worth mentioning, just some ancient cracks running far up the marble. Also a black tunnel carved in the stone wall that wandered off into illimitable gloom. The smell of rot and damp wafted to their nostrils.

Mygar poked his head in and pulled it back out, wincing with disgust. "Ew. Stinks down there. Like wet dog or something."

"Should we explore it?" suggested Svengar, studying its crudely rounded edges. "Could lead to some way outside this ruined temple."

"After you." He nudged his boot at the two dead men lying at their feet with cracked skulls. "Maybe it does and maybe it doesn't." The only other survivor swallowed the lump in his throat, the whites of his eyes little pinpricks of light, darting left and right in fear.

"How do you suppose the floor gave away?"

Mygar shrugged and gazed at the notched grooves inches from the top of the pit where the disappearing floor, the thin sheet of slate, had mysteriously slid aside. "Levers, tripwires, ropes weighted with blocks."

There came an eerie sound to their ears, like some claw or nail scraping on stone.

"What was that?" Mygar blurted. He whirled around.

Svengar just shook his head, sick with apprehension.

Another noise came. This one like a low growl. Some hellhound creeping through the dark. Mygar swallowed and shook his head, massaging his aching temple.

Mygar tensed, his fearful scowl betraying the fact he thought it was some predator. "Where does this damn, wretched tunnel lead? I've heard stories about ancient beasts, Svengar, kept hidden in these temples to punish the sinners. They'd sacrifice the blasphemers to them, then feast on their skulls during the full moon and commit rites to worship the god after the sacrifice was made."

Svengar scoffed. "That was ages ago, Mygar. You think these pansy-faced Driadis do-gooders would stoop to such atrocities? I doubt it. How long ago was it? What beast could—"

The growl came louder from the tunnel, and this time accompanied by clacking feet. Many feet.

Svengar drew the golden arrow back in the bowstrings and trained it at the black gap. He gave an audible gulp and the third man quailed at the lumbering shape of a troglodyte monster emerging from the tunnel. It was some hairy, four-legged thing with spikes protruding from a humped back like a monster porcupine. Svengar grew pale. The creature scurried forward, spider-like, with beady yellow eyes fixing on them like daggers; tusks, fangs outspread and curled back like a sickle.

Mygar thrust the rider forward. "Kill it."

"Me, lord. How shall—?"

"With your sword, you idiot. What else? Your nails, your teeth?"

"I don't think—"

Mygar kicked him forward. "Do it, man!" Svengar took aim. The arrow flew and plucked the beast in its side. It stuck out like one of its quills. Not a killing blow, the thing's hide was too thick for that, but it slowed it.

Not enough for their comrade to escape though. It hunched, tilted its spiny back and a volley of quills shot forth. It peppered the nearest man in the chest and face. He sagged back in agony. Some passed around his body and stuck in Mygar's arm. He gave a wild shriek. Another lodged in Svengar's boot, another in his lower leg, prompting a lurid howl. As they hopped about pulling out quills, the monster pounced on the fallen man, its teeth and tusks digging deep.

While the monster devoured its victim before their eyes, Mygar took a running leap, immune to the terrible screams and the blood. He springboarded off the monster's back to grapple for handholds in the cracks higher up on the wall. His fingers clawed the ancient stone and he pulled himself up over the lip while the wrathful beast swatted at his heels. It turned its attention to Svengar. The lieutenant gasped and dodged the giant hedgehog-like creature's claws, scrabbling his way up the wall, shredding nails and flesh. He willed his fingers to find handholds within the crumbling cracks like a cat with fire under its tail.

Mygar reached down and hauled the gibbering man up before the beast could tear at his heels. The two lay panting on the vine-ridden stone. The monster leapt up at them, snarling like a rabid dog, but the walls were too high and it couldn't reach them.

True to form, the magic that bound the arrow lifted it up and out from the monster's wound to roll at Svengar's side. The hedgehog thing swatted at the stone, blood slathering its ugly jowl. Its hunger was sated. Back it crept to the tunnel, leaving the mauled carcass of the huntsman behind on the bloody stone.

One by one Svengar and Mygar wiped the spittle from their

lips. They shook off the stink of death from their skin. "Let's go," mumbled Mygar. "We've lost our bows, but the outlanders have shown us a way out of here."

Svengar gusted a savage curse and began hewing at the vines with the knife strapped at his belt.

* * *

By and by, a band of Mygar's horsemen caught up with Mygar and his nephew who were leg-weary, blooded and ragged beyond recognition. They slumped by a stream of purling water in exhaustion.

"Lord, what is the meaning of this?" the lead rider called down to them.

"Fools. You could have come a little sooner."

"Lord, we tracked you—"

"Shut up, man. Give me your horse. Ride with Svengar. The others can't have gotten far on foot." His lips spread in a vengeful grimace. "There will be blood to pay and a terrible reckoning to come."

* * *

Far away in the direction of Caerlin, Risgan and the others struggled through the wilderness, over creeks, hollows and through untouched glades ringed with old growth. Ever did the denizens of the land survey the passing troupe with a feeling of strange curiosity, the great hares, owls, foxes and badger, for they felt fate hung in the balance and the woods would not be the same after the passing of these strange human folk. The isks had been ever circling the treetops, eager for blood, growing hungrier by the minute. The animals were wary of this; none could miss the baleful yellow eyes that sought the sight of fresh prey: those on foot rather than horse. Doubtless the isks had young to feed and many miles lay between them and their eyries. For the fugitives it was still a long way back to the village.

"Step it up, Hape," rasped Kahel.

"I'm moving as fast as I can, Kahel." Hape pulled up his brown robe, ragged and unkempt at the hem, trailing in the mud and the wet leaves from the recent rain.

A new sound greeted them. The thunder of hoofbeats. Risgan paled. There came with it a gleeful but vindictive promise of victory.

"There they are, lord!" shouted the lead scout with triumph. He reared in his saddle. "Just as I promised."

Jurna looked back with a growl of hate in his throat. "Now we're done for."

Arcadia raised her bow. She pegged off the first of the lead riders. At the writhing man's side, Mygar rode straight for her.

Arrows sang. Risgan and Kahel ducked and a horseman cut Jurna off and slashed a sword down at him. The blade clanged on Jurna's shiny steel. With a fierce yell he lunged in and smote the rider in the leg while another circled in to finish him off.

Moeze raised his silver disc. The talisman flared but the magic seemed to fizzle out with a raw hiss. Moeze cursed and looked at the disc with fury.

There came a rushing wind, like a funnel of disaster from the sky. In a chaos of whipping wings, the isks swooped. Like stormcrows of doom they whistled through the treetops, their talons raking away twitch leaves.

The horsemen wheeled aside, their roans and bays rearing in fright.

An anarchy of motion struck the small glade and Svengar's golden arrow went awry, catching Mygar in the leg. The chief gave a savage cry; he spilled from his mount, cursing in agony. Clutching at the shaft, he hobbled away, but was caught in the crossfire of Kahel's arrows and the fury of the isks. A giant bird, half black and half gray, landed in front of him and opened its beak wide. He lifted his sword, but the hulking creature clamped the blade in its beak, shook its massive head and flung the weapon off into the bushes.

Mygar's eyes mooned in terror. He bolted for the trees, but whatever hobbling strength he had was not enough to save him and the isk lifted wings after him and snatched at his sinewy bulk and bore him aloft. With a final wail to wake the dead he struggled, his legs kicking like a puppet dancing on a string.

"Fool!" cried Svengar, shaking a fist up at him. "See what happens when you don't kill your enemies!" Svengar was both anguished and gleeful at the sight of his uncle being carried off. His horse stumbled in a gopher hole, throwing him clear. He lay there in the wet leaves beating his fists on the ground in frustration, cursing the freak fall that had lamed his horse. He took hold of his senses and sucked in a breath. Clutching his bow and magic arrow, he grinned in maniacal triumph as a new reality surfaced in his mind.

He ran toward the knot of confusion, drawing his sword while Hape and Moeze scurried for safety. Three great isks dove to intercept, their shadows falling like lead weights over the woodland glade.

Risgan hastened in with a battle cry, smashing his club at a rider who tried to haul Arcadia away by the hair. Arcadia stuck an arrow in an isk that dove at Moeze. Crouching in disbelief, eyes blazing, she ducked a claw that swiped at her shoulders and loosed a shaft into the back of an unhorsed rider trying to despatch Jurna with a steely blade.

Svengar bellowed, "Isks take you all, fools! I control the wolf-brothers now. I'll usurp that weakling father of yours, unicorn lady. You'll become my new bride." He scrambled after Arcadia who scurried for safety after Risgan, Hape and Moeze while Kahel held the attackers back, shooting arrow after arrow into the midst of the winged horrors. Svengar laughed a wolf's laugh. "I'll break you in, you haughty—"

"Agh!" His boast was cut short as a sinister shadow loomed behind him and reaching claws grabbed his shoulders and hauled him aloft despite his fierce struggles. He shrieked once and the cry was torn from his throat. He ripped his sword from his scabbard and hacked again and again at the thing's talons, but nothing seemed to gouge that crusted bone and gristle that lurked under the hide of the elder isk.

Arcadia stared appalled at the humps of men slumping dead or twitching mortally wounded around her. Gray-black feathers floated in the air like dandelion fluff. "Wretches. Let me be free of this nightmare." In a last clutch at sanity, she stooped to seize the golden arrow that lay aside Svengar's fallen bow.

Risgan urged the others on, a great gash on his cheek under his left eye. "Leave the isks to their feast! Let us not join them." In desperation they rallied together and stumbled on through the trees, dreading to look back at that place of death.

The fate that awaited the two chiefs, dangling like wriggling worms in the claws of the mighty isks caused Risgan's heart to shudder.

Arcadia gripped the golden arrow in her hands. A sad look entered her eyes, as if the words of the goddess fled through her mind and gave her no comfort.

Ahead, the ageless trunks flanked them while an eerie maroon light filtered through the wavering boughs.

* * *

The exhausted party came to a halt before a woodland stream and drank deep of the cool water that flowed over rounded stones and down into a deep, jade-darkened pool. On they scrambled, through the sylvan depths, heedless of their wounds, fearing the return of the isks. Jurna sported a cut on his right arm where a huntsman's blade had sliced a thin, grazing stroke; Arcadia, Moeze and Hape nursed multiple bruises. Kahel had a gash over his right eye and a flap of skin hung loose on his arm where an isk's claw had gouged through his leathers.

They picked up their pace as the sun became a glimmering ball behind them and the woods a silent bastion of protection. Risgan marveled at their luck; they'd survived the isks and Mygar's attack, and the horror of being entombed in Driadis's lost temple. He also recalled the wish bone's magic and knew that it and the power of Driadis were behind them. He could not discount the enigmatic disappearance of the unicorn with the telltale blood smear on its flank at the temple's entranceway. The gloom had just swallowed it up. Where had it gone and how had it found that lost, fabled ruin?

Unless the unicorn and the goddess were one?

Moeze seemed to pick up on something of Risgan's restless thoughts.

"You can never conjure up a goddess, Risgan," he mumbled philosophically.

Kahel gave a skeptical snort. "If you're talking about that entity back at the temple, how do you know it was a goddess? I saw a shimmering apparition that could have been anything— even your magic for all we know."

"You're too much of a skeptic, Kahel," scoffed Hape. "When will you learn? You saw the unicorn as well as we did. It came back and led us to Driadis and lured Mygar there. He and his rogue lieutenant are dead, in the bellies of isks."

"All random happenings in my mind," grumbled Kahel. "Anything could have caused that."

"Oh?" Risgan laughed. "It could have been, Kahel, just plausible. Maybe."

"But somehow none of us think so," said Jurna.

Kahel just shrugged.

Arcadia nursed a doubtful frown.

On the way back to the village, as the fleeting light slanted between the swaying boughs, the company heard a soft whickering drift from the brush.

Jurna pointed between two massive twitch oaks. "Look, Kahel—your friend."

He gaped. "That miserable foal—" his eyes grew wide and shining. "I—"

The young unicorn reared on its hind legs, pawing at the air. Its deep blue eyes stared right at the archer. Perhaps a token of thanks for earlier deeds? The mother with the wounded side came out of the brush to stand beside it. It lifted its nose to sniff at the air.

Kahel shook his head.

"No need to speak, Kahel. Save it for your bedtime stories."

A slow grin crept over his hard-chiseled features. His red-bearded cheeks suddenly crinkled in mirth and he burst out in laughter: the second time in two weeks, a record for him.

"Come on, let's go," laughed Arcadia, while there's daylight about. I want to see you off on your journey."

* * *

The party approached Caerlin as the last light was fading, a much dog-eared troupe, dragging their feet and nursing aching bruises. What was left of Mygar's riders had not returned, still out looking for their master. It was just as well.

Arcadia cautioned them to silence and led the way forward. Past ghostly trunks and fallen logs. A voice called out of the shadows.

"Who goes there?"

Lokbur reined in, his sword flashing in his palm. His jaw

sagged when he saw Arcadia and he leapt off his roan to embrace her. "Arcadia, you have returned!"

Risgan saw his eyes blurred with what could have been tears. Relief and incomprehension were writ there, and something else. "I thought you were dead!" he cried.

"No, Lokbur, it'll take more than a few thugs like Mygar to kill me."

"Mygar—what's this talk? Everyone's looking for him."

"They won't find him."

"You mean he's—"

"Remember I am favored of the goddess. I have Driadis behind me."

Risgan bowed his head. "Only too true. Lady, we have completed our oath to you. We've seen you safely back to your village. Now, we'll take our leave, at least before your father gets second ideas about detaining us longer. As much as we like Caerlin, we do not want to spend the winter there."

"Of course. It goes without saying." She nodded and gestured to Lokbur to let them pass.

"Hold!" cried Lokbur. He held up a palm. "A parting gift—to you all."

"But—" Arcadia shook her head and caught up with him to whisper something in his ear and he nodded and whispered something back.

Risgan and his men gazed in puzzlement as he rode off back to the village.

While they huddled in the shrubs and as violet gloom crept about them, the huntsman returned bearing something with him.

He approached, out of breath, drawing a barrow-like cart behind him, supporting a square, thorned cage. "A little surprise for you," he said with a glint in his eye. The bars had been repaired and a small surly figure darted within, hissing and spitting.

"Afrid!" Jurna smacked a fist in palm. "Now there's a sight for sore eyes."

"I found the little witch skulking around Dodonis's hut earlier today, no doubt up to no good."

"Plotting some foul revenge on our good druid, I think," said Moeze.

"Good work, Lokbur. A relief." Risgan shook his head in amazement. "Now we're spared her midnight hexing."

"She's that bad?" Lokbur lifted brows.

"Worse."

"I think you'll want to say good-by to Thrulia too, Risgan?" Arcadia motioned to the bushes behind him.

He turned and gaped.

Another figure stepped out of the shadows, biding her time while the business of Afrid was squared up.

Risgan blinked and blushed. "How did you know?"

"You think we women are just dunces?" chided Arcadia. "I saw how she looked at you. No less how you looked at her."

Thrulia's doe eyes flashed. She held up food for them, venison and a pot of ale. Her face was flushed pink. "Risgan, good to see you."

"And you too, Lady. You are looking ravish—I mean, stunning, gorgeous as ever."

She curtsied and smiled. "And you as dashing as ever, relic hunter, despite the grime and cuts on your face and arms." She sighed. "In another life I would have taken you as my husband for your noble deeds—and not only that…" She scanned him from head to toe, and let her tongue flick over her lips. She halted her scrutiny and her eyes darted to her feet. "I'm not expecting you'll be staying?"

Risgan sighed, a low sibilant murmur. He held her in his arms. Gently he kissed her on the cheek. "No, milady, this is not the time. Certain deeds need attending to, involving a gem and a price on my head. In fact, the Pontific of Zanzuria is most displeased with the way I left town. There'll never be enough miles between me and his bounty hunters."

She nodded. "I understand." Although she likely didn't. "We thank you for all you have done. You've returned my sister, ever the mischief-maker she is."

"And you, Arcadia, what are you plans?" Risgan asked.

"Now that Mygar and his henchmen are no more, Lokbur and I will marry. I'll be damned if I let my father pawn Thrulia or me off in an arranged marriage ever again."

Lokbur and she looked in each other's eyes. They clasped each other again in a warm embrace.

Risgan peered through the trees and saw the village bonfire rising higher with fresh wood and torchlights gleaming and the scurrying of swift feet as if some great tension was in the air. "What will you do about the rest of Mygar's band?"

"We'll manage," said Arcadia. "Without a leader they'll be crippled and ineffective."

"I admire your spirit, Arcadia," Risgan murmured. "Why do I get the feeling you'll be the next queen of the Caerlin people before long?"

She grinned.

Lokbur lanced Arcadia a glowing look. They kissed in another heated embrace and all of Risgan's band clapped and laughed, even Kahel, the gruff Kahel.

Lokbur lifted a stern hand; his lips worked with emotion, as if he regretted their going. Arcadia was no less moved, her throat choked up, and a tear even came to Thrulia's eye. "Go, you outlaws, you have our blessings."

The mournful wail of the hunting horn echoed through the trees. "Quick! The rest of the Svengari hunters are coming! Back to the village. Take your witch and be gone. She's an omen around here."

Lokbur nodded. "Best to sneak out now while you can at dark."

"In those foul woods?" asked Moeze.

"I admit it is not ideal, but the consequences could be worse." Lokbur gave a brisk flourish. "Take the hidden path by the river, past the rapids. Then ford it over the stones at the place we call 'Milestone's Tomb'. That will get you far beyond any trackers our hetman may set after you."

Risgan nodded. "A good plan, Lokbur. Afrid may be getting a little wet, but so be it. Farewell." Wasting no time they made a beeline for the river, with Hape huffing, and Moeze mumbling and Risgan carting Afrid in tow.

The horn sounded again, and Risgan paused and turned to gaze back at Arcadia one more time. "Mistress," he called. "You're not a huntress any more, I can see it in your eyes. What will you do?"

She hesitated, rubbing her chin, licking her lower lip. She stepped over to address him personally. "I'll become a priestess, relic hunter, not like the pious ones that serve Dodonis. But one who devotes her energies to the stars and studying the animal mysteries. I'll help protect the sacred beasts. My allegiance lies with the unicorns. I'll bring them back. One day they will wander the forests without persecution from any hunters."

"My best wishes to you," said Risgan. Now it was his turn to pause. "But do priestesses marry? I thought they were supposed to be virgins?"

"I'll marry, Risgan, never fear!" she laughed. "I'm the priestess who makes her own rules. Even against my father's wishes. I will take over his rule one day. For now we must suffer through his blundering. But his power wanes every day and he will not last long as hetman. Then I will change the ways of the clan forever."

"You already have."

Long after Risgan and the others had taken to the trees, darkness spread over the land like a gloved hand. Risgan gave a long sigh.

"That's one noble and courageous lady."

"Yes," Jurna murmured, "too bad there weren't more of her kind."

Kahel lanced them a steely look. "Are you lugs going to yammer on, or shake a leg? The moon is up and I don't want to be picked off by any straggling isks."

ABOUT THE AUTHOR

Chris is a prolific author of fantasy, adventure, and science fiction. His writing spans many genres: heroic fantasy, sword and sorcery and speculative fiction.

Browse Chris's books at:

https://innersky.ca/books

The Upper Berth by F. Marion Crawford

Francis Marion Crawford was born on August 2nd, 1854 at Bagni di Lucca, Italy. An only son and a nephew to Julia Ward Howe, the American poet and writer of 'The Battle Hymn of the Republic'.

His education began at St Paul's School, Concord, New Hampshire, then to Cambridge University; University of Heidelberg; and the University of Rome.

In 1879 Crawford went to India, to study Sanskrit and then edited The Indian Herald. In 1881 he returned to America to continue his Sanskrit studies at Harvard University.

At this time in Boston he lived at his Aunt Julia house and in the company of his Uncle, Sam Ward. His family was concerned about his employment prospects. After a singing career as a baritone was ruled out, he was encouraged to write.

In December 1882 his first novel, 'Mr Isaacs', was an immediate hit which was amplified by 'Dr Claudius' in 1883.

In October 1884 he married Elizabeth Berdan. They went on to have two sons and two daughters.

Encouraged by his excellent start to a literary career he returned to Italy with Elizabeth to make a permanent home, principally in Sant' Agnello, where he bought the Villa Renzi that then became Villa Crawford.

In the late 1890s, he began to write his historical works: 'Ave Roma Immortalis' (1898), 'Rulers of the South' (1900) and 'Gleanings from Venetian History' (1905). The Saracinesca series is perhaps his best work. 'Saracinesca' was followed by 'Sant' Ilario' in 1889, 'Don Orsino' in 1892 and 'Corleone' in 1897, that being the first major treatment of the Mafia in literature.

Francis Marion Crawford died at Sorrento on Good Friday 1909 at Villa Crawford of a heart attack.

Index of Contents
I - THE UPPER BERTH
II - BY THE WATERS OF PARADISE
F. MARION CRAWFORD – A SHORT BIOGRAPHY
F. MARION CRAWFORD – A CONCISE BIBLIOGRAPHY

THE UPPER BERTH

I

Somebody asked for the cigars. We had talked long, and the conversation was beginning to languish; the tobacco smoke had got into the heavy curtains, the wine had got into those brains which were liable to become heavy, and it was already perfectly evident that, unless somebody did something to rouse our oppressed spirits, the meeting would soon come to its natural conclusion, and we, the guests, would speedily go home to bed, and most certainly to sleep. No one had said anything very remarkable; it may be that no one had anything very remarkable to say. Jones had given us every particular of his last hunting adventure in Yorkshire. Mr. Tompkins, of Boston, had explained at elaborate length those working principles, by the due and careful maintenance of which the Atchison, Topeka, and Santa Fé Railroad not only extended its territory, increased its departmental influence, and transported live stock without starving them to death before the day of actual delivery, but, also, had for years succeeded in deceiving those passengers who bought its tickets into the fallacious belief that the corporation aforesaid was really able to transport human life without destroying it. Signor Tombola had endeavoured to persuade us, by arguments which we took no trouble to oppose, that the unity of his country in no way resembled the average modern torpedo, carefully planned, constructed with all the skill of the greatest European arsenals, but, when constructed, destined to be directed by feeble hands into a region where it must undoubtedly explode, unseen, unfeared, and unheard, into the illimitable wastes of political chaos.

It is unnecessary to go into further details. The conversation had assumed proportions which would have bored Prometheus on his rock, which would have driven Tantalus to distraction, and which would have impelled Ixion to seek relaxation in the simple but instructive dialogues of Herr Ollendorff, rather than submit to the greater evil of listening to our talk. We had sat at table for hours; we were bored, we were tired, and nobody showed signs of moving.

Somebody called for cigars. We all instinctively looked towards the speaker. Brisbane was a man of five-and-thirty years of age, and remarkable for those gifts which chiefly attract the attention of men. He was a strong man. The external proportions of his figure presented nothing extraordinary to the common eye, though his size was above the average. He was a little over six feet in height, and moderately broad in the shoulder; he did not appear to be stout, but, on the other hand, he was certainly not thin; his small head was supported by a strong and sinewy neck; his broad muscular hands appeared to possess a peculiar skill in breaking walnuts without the assistance of the ordinary cracker, and, seeing him in profile, one could not help remarking the extraordinary breadth of his sleeves, and the unusual thickness of his chest. He was one of those men who are commonly spoken of among men as deceptive; that is to say, that though he looked exceedingly strong he was in reality very much stronger than he looked. Of his features I need say little. His head is small, his hair is thin, his eyes are blue, his nose is large, he has a small moustache, and a square jaw. Everybody knows Brisbane, and when he asked for a cigar everybody looked at him.

"It is a very singular thing," said Brisbane.

Everybody stopped talking. Brisbane's voice was not loud, but possessed a peculiar quality of penetrating general conversation, and cutting it like a knife. Everybody listened. Brisbane, perceiving that he had attracted their general attention, lit his cigar with great equanimity.

"It is very singular," he continued, "that thing about ghosts. People are always asking whether anybody has seen a ghost. I have."

"Bosh! What, you? You don't mean to say so, Brisbane? Well, for a man of his intelligence!"

A chorus of exclamations greeted Brisbane's remarkable statement. Everybody called for cigars, and Stubbs the butler suddenly appeared from the depths of nowhere with a fresh bottle of dry champagne. The situation was saved; Brisbane was going to tell a story.

I am an old sailor, said Brisbane, and as I have to cross the Atlantic pretty often, I have my favourites. Most men have their favourites. I have seen a man wait in a Broadway bar for three-quarters of an hour for a particular car which he liked. I believe the bar-keeper made at least one-third of his living by that man's preference. I have a habit of waiting for certain ships when I am obliged to cross that duck-pond. It may be a prejudice, but I was never cheated out of a good passage but once in my life. I remember it very well; it was a warm morning in June, and the Custom House officials, who were hanging about waiting for a steamer already on her way up from the Quarantine, presented a peculiarly hazy and thoughtful appearance. I had not much luggage—I never have. I mingled with the crowd of passengers, porters, and officious individuals in blue coats and brass buttons, who seemed to spring up like mushrooms from the deck of a moored steamer to obtrude their unnecessary services upon the independent passenger. I have often noticed with a certain interest the spontaneous evolution of these fellows. They are not there when you arrive; five minutes after the pilot has called "Go ahead!" they, or at least their blue coats and brass buttons, have disappeared from deck and gangway as completely as though they had been consigned to that locker which tradition unanimously ascribes to Davy Jones. But, at the moment of starting, they are there, clean-shaved, blue-coated, and ravenous for fees. I hastened on board. The Kamtschatka was one of my favourite ships. I say was, because she emphatically no longer is. I cannot conceive of any inducement which could entice me to make another voyage in her. Yes, I know what you are going to say. She is uncommonly clean in the run aft, she has enough bluffing off in the bows to keep her dry, and the lower berths are most of them double. She has a lot of advantages, but I won't cross in her again. Excuse the digression. I got on board. I hailed a steward, whose red nose and redder whiskers were equally familiar to me.

"One hundred and five, lower berth," said I, in the businesslike tone peculiar to men who think no more of crossing the Atlantic than taking a whisky cocktail at downtown Delmonico's.

The steward took my portmanteau, great coat, and rug. I shall never forget the expression of his face. Not that he turned pale. It is maintained by the most eminent divines that even miracles cannot change the course of nature. I have no hesitation in saying that he did not turn pale; but, from his expression, I judged that he was either about to shed tears, to sneeze, or to drop my portmanteau. As the latter contained two bottles of particularly fine old sherry presented to me for my voyage by my old friend Snigginson van Pickyns, I felt extremely nervous. But the steward did none of these things.

"Well, I'm d—d!" said he in a low voice, and led the way.

I supposed my Hermes, as he led me to the lower regions, had had a little grog, but I said nothing, and followed him. One hundred and five was on the port side, well aft. There was nothing remarkable about the state-room. The lower berth, like most of those upon the Kamtschatka, was double. There was plenty of room; there was the usual washing apparatus, calculated to convey an idea of luxury to the mind of a North-American Indian; there were the usual inefficient racks of brown wood, in which it is more easy to hang a large-sized umbrella than the common tooth-brush of commerce. Upon the uninviting mattresses were carefully folded together those blankets which a great modern humorist has aptly compared to cold buckwheat cakes. The question of towels was left entirely to the imagination. The glass decanters were filled with a transparent liquid faintly tinged with brown, but from which an odor less faint, but not more pleasing, ascended to the nostrils, like a far-off sea-sick reminiscence of oily machinery. Sad-coloured curtains half-closed the upper berth. The hazy June daylight shed a faint illumination upon the desolate little scene. Ugh! how I hate that state-room!

The steward deposited my traps and looked at me, as though he wanted to get away—probably in search of more passengers and more fees. It is always a good plan to start in favour with those functionaries, and I accordingly gave him certain coins there and then.

"I'll try and make yer comfortable all I can," he remarked, as he put the coins in his pocket. Nevertheless, there was a doubtful intonation in his voice which surprised me. Possibly his scale of fees had gone up, and he was not satisfied; but on the whole I was inclined to think that, as he himself would have expressed it, he was "the better for a glass." I was wrong, however, and did the man injustice.

II

Nothing especially worthy of mention occurred during that day. We left the pier punctually, and it was very pleasant to be fairly under way, for the weather was warm and sultry, and the motion of the steamer produced a refreshing breeze. Everybody knows what the first day at sea is like. People pace the decks and stare at each other, and occasionally meet acquaintances whom they did not know to be on board. There is the usual uncertainty as to whether the food will be good, bad, or indifferent, until the first two meals have put the matter beyond a doubt; there is the usual uncertainty about the weather, until the ship is fairly off Fire Island. The tables are crowded at first, and then suddenly thinned. Pale-faced people spring from their seats and precipitate themselves towards the door, and each old sailor breathes more freely as his sea-sick neighbour rushes from his side, leaving him plenty of elbow room and an unlimited command over the mustard.

One passage across the Atlantic is very much like another, and we who cross very often do not make the voyage for the sake of novelty. Whales and icebergs are indeed always objects of interest, but, after all, one whale is very much like another whale, and one rarely sees an iceberg at close quarters. To the majority of us the most delightful moment of the day on board an ocean steamer is when we have taken our last turn on deck, have smoked our last cigar, and having succeeded in tiring ourselves, feel at liberty to turn in with a clear conscience. On that first night of the voyage I felt particularly lazy, and went to bed in one hundred and five rather earlier than I usually do. As I turned in, I was amazed to see that I was to have a companion. A portmanteau, very like my own, lay in the opposite corner, and in the upper berth had been deposited a neatly folded rug with a stick and umbrella. I had hoped to be alone, and I was disappointed; but I wondered who my room-mate was to be, and I determined to have a look at him.

Before I had been long in bed he entered. He was, as far as I could see, a very tall man, very thin, very pale, with sandy hair and whiskers and colourless grey eyes. He had about him, I thought, an air of rather dubious fashion; the sort of man you might see in Wall Street, without being able precisely to say what he was doing there—the sort of man who frequents the Café Anglais, who always seems to be alone and who drinks champagne; you might meet him on a race-course, but he would never appear to be doing anything there either. A little over-dressed—a little odd. There are three or four of his kind on every ocean steamer. I made up my mind that I did not care to make his acquaintance, and I went to sleep saying to myself that I would study his habits in order to avoid him. If he rose early, I would rise late; if he went to bed late, I would go to bed early. I did not care to know him. If you once know people of that kind they are always turning up. Poor fellow! I need not have taken the trouble to come to so many decisions about him, for I never saw him again after that first night in one hundred and five.

I was sleeping soundly when I was suddenly waked by a loud noise. To judge from the sound, my room-mate must have sprung with a single leap from the upper berth to the floor. I heard him fumbling with the latch and bolt of the door, which opened almost immediately, and then I heard his footsteps as he ran at full speed down the passage, leaving the door open behind him. The ship was rolling a little, and I expected to hear him stumble or fall, but he ran as though he were running for his life. The door swung on its hinges with the motion of the vessel, and the sound annoyed me. I got up and shut it, and groped my way back to my berth in the darkness. I went to sleep again; but I have no idea how long I slept.

When I awoke it was still quite dark, but I felt a disagreeable sensation of cold, and it seemed to me that the air was damp. You know the peculiar smell of a cabin which has been wet with sea water. I covered myself up as well as I could and dozed off again, framing complaints to be made the next day, and selecting the most powerful epithets in the language. I could hear my room-mate turn over in the upper berth. He had probably returned while I was asleep. Once I thought I heard him groan, and I argued that he was sea-sick. That is particularly unpleasant when one is below. Nevertheless I dozed off and slept till early daylight.

The ship was rolling heavily, much more than on the previous evening, and the grey light which came in through the porthole changed in tint with every movement according as the angle of the vessel's side turned the glass seawards or skywards. It was very cold—unaccountably so for the month of June. I turned my head and looked at the porthole, and saw to my surprise that it was wide open and hooked back. I believe I swore audibly. Then I got up and shut it. As I turned back I glanced at the upper berth. The curtains were drawn close together; my companion had probably felt cold as well as I. It struck me that I had slept enough. The state-room was uncomfortable, though, strange to say, I could not smell the dampness which had annoyed me in the night. My room-mate was still asleep—excellent opportunity for avoiding him, so I dressed at once and went on deck. The day was warm and cloudy, with an oily smell on the water. It was seven o'clock as I came out—much later than I had imagined. I came across the doctor, who was taking his first sniff of the morning air. He was a young man from the West of Ireland—a tremendous fellow, with black hair and blue eyes, already inclined to be stout; he had a happy-go-lucky, healthy look about him which was rather attractive.

"Fine morning," I remarked, by way of introduction.

"Well," said he, eying me with an air of ready interest, "it's a fine morning and it's not a fine morning. I don't think it's much of a morning."

"Well, no—it is not so very fine," said I.

"It's just what I call fuggly weather," replied the doctor.

"It was very cold last night, I thought," I remarked. "However, when I looked about, I found that the porthole was wide open. I had not noticed it when I went to bed. And the state-room was damp, too."

"Damp!" said he. "Whereabouts are you?"

"One hundred and five—"

To my surprise the doctor started visibly, and stared at me.

"What is the matter?" I asked.

"Oh—nothing," he answered; "only everybody has complained of that state-room for the last three trips."

"I shall complain too," I said. "It has certainly not been properly aired. It is a shame!"

"I don't believe it can be helped," answered the doctor. "I believe there is something—well, it is not my business to frighten passengers."

"You need not be afraid of frightening me," I replied. "I can stand any amount of damp. If I should get a bad cold I will come to you."

I offered the doctor a cigar, which he took and examined very critically.

"It is not so much the damp," he remarked. "However, I dare say you will get on very well. Have you a room-mate?"

"Yes; a deuce of a fellow, who bolts out in the middle of the night and leaves the door open."

Again the doctor glanced curiously at me. Then he lit the cigar and looked grave.

"Did he come back?" he asked presently.

"Yes. I was asleep, but I waked up and heard him moving. Then I felt cold and went to sleep again. This morning I found the porthole open."

"Look here," said the doctor, quietly, "I don't care much for this ship. I don't care a rap for her reputation. I tell you what I will do. I have a good-sized place up here. I will share it with you, though I don't know you from Adam."

I was very much surprised at the proposition. I could not imagine why he should take such a sudden interest in my welfare. However, his manner as he spoke of the ship was peculiar.

"You are very good, doctor," I said. "But really, I believe even now the cabin could be aired, or cleaned out, or something. Why do you not care for the ship?"

"We are not superstitious in our profession, sir," replied the doctor. "But the sea makes people so. I don't want to prejudice you, and I don't want to frighten you, but if you will take my advice you will move in here. I would as soon see you overboard," he added, "as know that you or any other man was to sleep in one hundred and five."

"Good gracious! Why?" I asked.

"Just because on the last three trips the people who have slept there actually have gone overboard," he answered, gravely.

The intelligence was startling and exceedingly unpleasant, I confess. I looked hard at the doctor to see whether he was making game of me, but he looked perfectly serious. I thanked him warmly for his offer, but told him I intended to be the exception to the rule by which every one who slept in that particular state-room went overboard. He did not say much, but looked as grave as ever, and hinted that before we got across I should probably reconsider his proposal. In the course of time we went to breakfast, at which only an inconsiderable number of passengers assembled. I noticed that one or two of the officers who breakfasted with us looked grave. After breakfast I went into my state-room in order to get a book. The curtains of the upper berth were still closely drawn. Not a word was to be heard. My room-mate was probably still asleep.

As I came out I met the steward whose business it was to look after me. He whispered that the captain wanted to see me, and then scuttled away down the passage as if very anxious to avoid any questions. I went toward the captain's cabin, and found him waiting for me.

"Sir," said he, "I want to ask a favour of you."

I answered that I would do anything to oblige him.

"Your room-mate has disappeared," he said. "He is known to have turned in early last night. Did you notice anything extraordinary in his manner?"

The question coming, as it did, in exact confirmation of the fears the doctor had expressed half an hour earlier, staggered me.

"You don't mean to say he has gone overboard?" I asked.

"I fear he has," answered the captain.

"This is the most extraordinary thing—" I began.

"Why?" he asked.

"He is the fourth, then?" I explained. In answer to another question from the captain, I explained, without mentioning the doctor, that I had heard the story concerning one hundred and five. He seemed very much annoyed at hearing that I knew of it. I told him what had occurred in the night.

"What you say," he replied, "coincides almost exactly with what was told me by the room-mates of two of the other three. They bolt out of bed and run down the passage. Two of them were seen to go overboard by the watch; we stopped and lowered boats, but they were not found. Nobody, however, saw or heard the man who was lost last night—if he is really lost. The steward, who is a superstitious fellow, perhaps, and expected something to go wrong, went to look for him this morning, and found his berth empty, but his clothes lying about, just as he had left them. The steward was the only man on board who knew him by sight, and he has been searching everywhere for him. He has disappeared! Now, sir, I want to beg you not to mention the circumstance to any of the passengers; I don't want the ship to get a bad name, and nothing hangs about an ocean-goer like stories of suicides. You shall have your choice of any one of the officers' cabins you like, including my own, for the rest of the passage. Is that a fair bargain?"

"Very," said I; "and I am much obliged to you. But since I am alone, and have the state-room to myself, I would rather not move. If the steward will take out that unfortunate man's things, I would as leave stay where I am. I will not say anything about the matter, and I think I can promise you that I will not follow my room-mate."

The captain tried to dissuade me from my intention, but I preferred having a state-room alone to being the chum of any officer on board. I do not know whether I acted foolishly, but if I had taken his advice I should have had nothing more to tell. There would have remained the disagreeable coincidence of several suicides occurring among men who had slept in the same cabin, but that would have been all.

That was not the end of the matter, however, by any means. I obstinately made up my mind that I would not be disturbed by such tales, and I even went so far as to argue the question with the captain. There was something wrong about the state-room, I said. It was rather damp. The porthole had been left open last night. My room-mate might have been ill when he came on board, and he might have become delirious after he went to bed. He might even now be hiding somewhere on board, and might be found later. The place ought to be aired and the fastening of the port looked to. If the captain would give me leave, I would see that what I thought necessary were done immediately.

"Of course you have a right to stay where you are if you please," he replied, rather petulantly; "but I wish you would turn out and let me lock the place up, and be done with it."

I did not see it in the same light, and left the captain, after promising to be silent concerning the disappearance of my companion. The latter had had no acquaintances on board, and was not missed in the course of the day. Towards evening I met the doctor again, and he asked me whether I had changed my mind. I told him I had not.

"Then you will before long," he said, very gravely.

III

We played whist in the evening, and I went to bed late. I will confess now that I felt a disagreeable sensation when I entered my state-room. I could not help thinking of the tall man I had seen on the previous night, who was now dead, drowned, tossing about in the long swell, two or three hundred miles astern. His face rose very distinctly before me as I undressed, and I even went so far as to draw back the curtains of the upper berth, as though to persuade myself that he was actually gone. I also bolted the door of the state-room. Suddenly I became aware that the porthole was open, and fastened back. This was more than I could stand. I hastily threw on my dressing-gown and went in search of Robert, the steward of my passage. I was very angry, I remember, and when I found him I dragged him roughly to the door of one hundred and five, and pushed him towards the open porthole.

"What the deuce do you mean, you scoundrel, by leaving that port open every night? Don't you know it is against the regulations? Don't you know that if the ship heeled and the water began to come in, ten men could not shut it? I will report you to the captain, you blackguard, for endangering the ship!"

I was exceedingly wroth. The man trembled and turned pale, and then began to shut the round glass plate with the heavy brass fittings.

"Why don't you answer me?" I said, roughly.

"If you please, sir," faltered Robert, "there's nobody on board as can keep this 'ere port shut at night. You can try it yourself, sir. I ain't a-going to stop hany longer on board o' this vessel, sir; I ain't, indeed. But if I was you, sir, I'd just clear out and go and sleep with the surgeon, or something, I would. Look 'ere, sir, is that fastened what you may call securely, or not, sir? Try it, sir, see if it will move a hinch."

I tried the port, and found it perfectly tight.

"Well, sir," continued Robert, triumphantly, "I wager my reputation as a A1 steward, that in 'arf an hour it will be open again; fastened back, too, sir, that's the horful thing—fastened back!"

I examined the great screw and the looped nut that ran on it.

"If I find it open in the night, Robert, I will give you a sovereign. It is not possible. You may go."

"Soverin' did you say, sir? Very good, sir. Thank ye, sir. Good night, sir. Pleasant reepose, sir, and all manner of hinchantin' dreams, sir."

Robert scuttled away, delighted at being released. Of course, I thought he was trying to account for his negligence by a silly story, intended to frighten me, and I disbelieved him. The consequence was that he got his sovereign, and I spent a very peculiarly unpleasant night.

I went to bed, and five minutes after I had rolled myself up in my blankets the inexorable Robert extinguished the light that burned steadily behind the ground-glass pane near the door. I lay quite still in the dark trying to go to sleep, but I soon found that impossible. It had been some satisfaction to be angry with the steward, and the diversion had banished that unpleasant sensation I had at first experienced when I thought of the drowned man who had been my chum; but I was no longer sleepy, and I lay awake for some time, occasionally glancing at the porthole, which I could just see from where I lay, and which, in the darkness, looked like a faintly-luminous soup-plate suspended in blackness. I believe I must have lain there for an hour, and, as I remember, I was just dozing into sleep when I was roused by a draught of cold air and by distinctly feeling the spray of the sea blown upon my face. I started to my feet, and not having allowed in the dark for the motion of the ship, I was instantly thrown violently across the state-room upon the couch which was placed beneath the porthole. I recovered myself immediately, however, and climbed upon my knees. The porthole was again wide open and fastened back!

Now these things are facts. I was wide awake when I got up, and I should certainly have been waked by the fall had I still been dozing. Moreover, I bruised my elbows and knees badly, and the bruises were there on the following morning to testify to the fact, if I myself had doubted it. The porthole was wide open and fastened back—a thing so unaccountable that I remember very well feeling astonishment rather than fear when I discovered it. I at once closed the plate again and screwed down the loop nut with all my strength. It was very dark in the state-room. I reflected that the port had certainly been opened within an hour after Robert had at first shut it in my presence, and I determined to watch it and see whether it would open again. Those brass fittings are very heavy and by no means easy to move; I could not believe that the clump had been turned by the shaking of the screw. I stood peering out through the thick glass at the alternate white and grey streaks of the sea that foamed beneath the ship's side. I must have remained there a quarter of an hour.

Suddenly, as I stood, I distinctly heard something moving behind me in one of the berths, and a moment afterwards, just as I turned instinctively to look—though I could, of course, see nothing in the darkness—I heard a very faint groan. I sprang across the state-room, and tore the curtains of the upper berth aside, thrusting in my hands to discover if there were any one there. There was some one.

I remember that the sensation as I put my hands forward was as though I were plunging them into the air of a damp cellar, and from behind the curtain came a gust of wind that smelled horribly of stagnant sea-water. I laid hold of something that had the shape of a man's arm, but was smooth, and wet, and icy cold. But suddenly, as I pulled, the creature sprang violently forward against me, a clammy, oozy mass, as it seemed to me, heavy and wet, yet endowed with a sort of supernatural strength. I reeled across the state-room, and in an instant the door opened and the thing rushed out. I had not had time to be frightened, and quickly recovering myself, I sprang through the door and gave chase at the top of my speed, but I was too late. Ten yards before me I could see—I am sure I saw it—a dark shadow moving in the dimly lighted passage, quickly as the shadow of a fast horse thrown before a dog-cart by the lamp on a dark night. But in a moment it had disappeared, and I found myself holding on to the polished rail that ran along the bulkhead where the passage turned towards the companion. My hair stood on end, and the cold perspiration rolled down my face. I am not ashamed of it in the least: I was very badly frightened.

Still I doubted my senses, and pulled myself together. It was absurd, I thought. The Welsh rare-bit I had eaten had disagreed with me. I had been in a nightmare. I made my way back to my state-room, and entered it with an effort. The whole place smelled of stagnant sea-water, as it had when I had waked on the previous evening. It required my utmost strength to go in and grope among my things for a box of wax lights. As I lighted a railway reading lantern which I always carry in case I want to read after the lamps are out, I perceived that the porthole was again open, and a sort of creeping horror began to take possession of me which I never felt before, nor wish to feel again. But I got a light and proceeded to examine the upper berth, expecting to find it drenched with sea-water.

But I was disappointed. The bed had been slept in, and the smell of the sea was strong; but the bedding was as dry as a bone. I fancied that Robert had not had the courage to make the bed after the accident of the previous night—it had all been a hideous dream. I drew the curtains back as far as I could and examined the place very carefully. It was perfectly dry. But the porthole was open again. With a sort of dull bewilderment of horror, I closed it and screwed it down, and thrusting my heavy stick through the brass loop, wrenched it with all my might, till the thick metal began to bend under the pressure. Then I hooked my reading lantern into the red velvet at the head of the couch, and sat down to recover my senses if I could. I sat there all night, unable to think of rest—hardly able to think at all. But the porthole remained closed, and I did not believe it would now open again without the application of a considerable force.

The morning dawned at last, and I dressed myself slowly, thinking over all that had happened in the night. It was a beautiful day and I went on deck, glad to get out in the early, pure sunshine, and to smell the breeze from the blue water, so different from the noisome, stagnant odour from my state-room. Instinctively I turned aft, towards the surgeon's cabin. There he stood, with a pipe in his mouth, taking his morning airing precisely as on the preceding day.

"Good-morning," said he, quietly, but looking at me with evident curiosity.

"Doctor, you were quite right," said I. "There is something wrong about that place."

"I thought you would change your mind," he answered, rather triumphantly. "You have had a bad night, eh? Shall I make you a pick-me-up? I have a capital recipe."

"No, thanks," I cried. "But I would like to tell you what happened."

I then tried to explain as clearly as possible precisely what had occurred, not omitting to state that I had been scared as I had never been scared in my whole life before. I dwelt particularly on the phenomenon of the porthole, which was a fact to which I could testify, even if the rest had been an illusion. I had closed it twice in the night, and the second time I had actually bent the brass in wrenching it with my stick. I believe I insisted a good deal on this point.

"You seem to think I am likely to doubt the story," said the doctor, smiling at the detailed account of the state of the porthole. "I do not doubt it in the least. I renew my invitation to you. Bring your traps here, and take half my cabin."

"Come and take half of mine for one night," I said. "Help me to get at the bottom of this thing."

"You will get to the bottom of something else if you try," answered the doctor.

"What?" I asked.

"The bottom of the sea. I am going to leave the ship. It is not canny."

"Then you will not help me to find out—"

"Not I," said the doctor, quickly. "It is my business to keep my wits about me—not to go fiddling about with ghosts and things."

"Do you really believe it is a ghost?" I inquired, rather contemptuously. But as I spoke I remembered very well the horrible sensation of the supernatural which had got possession of me during the night. The doctor turned sharply on me—

"Have you any reasonable explanation of these things to offer?" he asked. "No; you have not. Well, you say you will find an explanation. I say that you won't, sir, simply because there is not any."

"But, my dear sir," I retorted, "do you, a man of science, mean to tell me that such things cannot be explained?"

"I do," he answered, stoutly. "And, if they could, I would not be concerned in the explanation."

I did not care to spend another night alone in the state-room, and yet I was obstinately determined to get at the root of the disturbances. I do not believe there are many men who would have slept there alone, after passing two such nights. But I made up my mind to try it, if I could not get any one to share a watch with me. The doctor was evidently not inclined for such an experiment. He said he was a surgeon, and that in case any accident occurred on board he must always be in readiness. He could not afford to have his nerves unsettled. Perhaps he was quite right, but I am inclined to think that his precaution was prompted by his inclination. On inquiry, he informed me that there was no one on board who would be likely to join me in my investigations, and after a little more conversation I left him. A little later I met the captain, and told him my story. I said that if no one would spend the night with me I would ask leave to have the light burning all night, and would try it alone.

"Look here," said he, "I will tell you what I will do. I will share your watch myself, and we will see what happens. It is my belief that we can find out between us. There may be some fellow skulking on board, who steals a passage by frightening the passengers. It is just possible that there may be something queer in the carpentering of that berth."

I suggested taking the ship's carpenter below and examining the place; but I was overjoyed at the captain's offer to spend the night with me. He accordingly sent for the workman and ordered him to do anything I required. We went below at once. I had all the bedding cleared out of the upper berth, and we examined the place thoroughly to see if there was a board loose anywhere, or a panel which could be opened or pushed aside. We tried the planks everywhere, tapped the flooring, unscrewed the fittings of the lower berth and took it to pieces—in short, there was not a square inch of the state-room which was not searched and tested. Everything was in perfect order, and we put everything back in its place. As we were finishing our work, Robert came to the door and looked in.

"Well, sir—find anything, sir?" he asked with a ghastly grin.

"You were right about the porthole, Robert," I said, and I gave him the promised sovereign. The carpenter did his work silently and skilfully, following my directions. When he had done he spoke.

"I'm a plain man, sir," he said. "But it's my belief you had better just turn out your things and let me run half a dozen four inch screws through the door of this cabin. There's no good never came o' this cabin yet, sir, and that's all about it. There's been four lives lost out o' here to my own remembrance, and that in four trips. Better give it up, sir—better give it up!"

"I will try it for one night more," I said.

"Better give it up, sir—better give it up! It's a precious bad job," repeated the workman, putting his tools in his bag and leaving the cabin.

But my spirits had risen considerably at the prospect of having the captain's company, and I made up my mind not to be prevented from going to the end of the strange business. I abstained from Welsh rare-bits and grog that evening, and did not even join in the customary game of whist. I wanted to be quite sure of my nerves, and my vanity made me anxious to make a good figure in the captain's eyes.

IV

The captain was one of those splendidly tough and cheerful specimens of seafaring humanity whose combined courage, hardihood, and calmness in difficulty leads them naturally into high positions of trust. He was not the man to be led away by an idle tale, and the mere fact that he was willing to join me in the investigation was proof that he thought there was something seriously wrong, which could not be accounted for on ordinary theories, nor laughed down as a common superstition. To some extent, too, his reputation was at stake, as well as the reputation of the ship. It is no light thing to lose passengers overboard, and he knew it.

About ten o'clock that evening, as I was smoking a last cigar, he came up to me and drew me aside from the beat of the other passengers who were patrolling the deck in the warm darkness.

"This is a serious matter, Mr. Brisbane," he said. "We must make up our minds either way—to be disappointed or to have a pretty rough time of it. You see, I cannot afford to laugh at the affair, and I will ask you to sign your name to a statement of whatever occurs. If nothing happens to-night we will try it again to-morrow and next day. Are you ready?"

So we went below, and entered the state-room. As we went in I could see Robert the steward, who stood a little further down the passage, watching us, with his usual grin, as though certain that something dreadful was about to happen. The captain closed the door behind us and bolted it.

"Supposing we put your portmanteau before the door," he suggested. "One of us can sit on it. Nothing can get out then. Is the port screwed down?"

I found it as I had left it in the morning. Indeed, without using a lever, as I had done, no one could have opened it. I drew back the curtains of the upper berth so that I could see well into it. By the captain's advice I lighted my reading-lantern, and placed it so that it shone upon the white sheets above. He insisted upon sitting on the portmanteau, declaring that he wished to be able to swear that he had sat before the door.

Then he requested me to search the state-room thoroughly, an operation very soon accomplished, as it consisted merely in looking beneath the lower berth and under the couch below the porthole. The spaces were quite empty.

"It is impossible for any human being to get in," I said, "or for any human being to open the port."

"Very good," said the captain, calmly. "If we see anything now, it must be either imagination or something supernatural."

I sat down on the edge of the lower berth.

"The first time it happened," said the captain, crossing his legs and leaning back against the door, "was in March. The passenger who slept here, in the upper berth, turned out to have been a lunatic—at all events, he was known to have been a little touched, and he had taken his passage without the knowledge of his friends. He rushed out in the middle of the night, and threw himself overboard, before the officer who had the watch could stop him. We stopped and lowered a boat; it was a quiet night, just before that heavy weather came on; but we could not find him. Of course his suicide was afterwards accounted for on the ground of his insanity."

"I suppose that often happens?" I remarked, rather absently.

"Not often—no," said the captain; "never before in my experience, though I have heard of it happening on board of other ships. Well, as I was saying, that occurred in March. On the very next trip—What are you looking at?" he asked, stopping suddenly in his narration.

I believe I gave no answer. My eyes were riveted upon the porthole. It seemed to me that the brass loop-nut was beginning to turn very slowly upon the screw—so slowly, however, that I was not sure it moved at all. I watched it intently, fixing its position in my mind, and trying to ascertain whether it changed. Seeing where I was looking, the captain looked too.

"It moves!" he exclaimed, in a tone of conviction. "No, it does not," he added, after a minute.

"If it were the jarring of the screw," said I, "it would have opened during the day; but I found it this evening jammed tight as I left it this morning."

I rose and tried the nut. It was certainly loosened, for by an effort I could move it with my hands.

"The queer thing," said the captain, "is that the second man who was lost is supposed to have got through that very port. We had a terrible time over it. It was in the middle of the night, and the weather was very heavy; there was an alarm that one of the ports was open and the sea running in. I came below and found everything flooded, the water pouring in every time she rolled, and the whole port swinging from the top bolts—not the porthole in the middle. Well, we managed to shut it, but the water did some damage. Ever since that the place smells of sea-water from time to time. We supposed the passenger had thrown himself out, though the Lord only knows how he did it. The steward kept telling me that he could not keep anything shut here. Upon my word—I can smell it now, cannot you?" he inquired, sniffing the air suspiciously.

"Yes—distinctly," I said, and I shuddered as that same odour of stagnant sea-water grew stronger in the cabin. "Now, to smell like this, the place must be damp," I continued, "and yet when I examined it with the carpenter this morning everything was perfectly dry. It is most extraordinary—hallo!"

My reading-lantern, which had been placed in the upper berth, was suddenly extinguished. There was still a good deal of light from the pane of ground glass near the door, behind which loomed the regulation lamp. The ship rolled heavily, and the curtain of the upper berth swung far out into the state-room and back again. I rose quickly from my seat on the edge of the bed, and the captain at the same moment started to his feet with a loud cry of surprise. I had turned with the intention of taking down the lantern to examine it, when I heard his exclamation, and immediately afterwards his call for help. I sprang towards him. He was wrestling with all his might, with the brass loop of the port. It seemed to turn against his hands in spite of all his efforts. I caught up my cane, a heavy oak stick I always used to carry, and thrust it through the ring and bore on it with all my strength. But the strong wood snapped suddenly, and I fell upon the couch. When I rose again the port was wide open, and the captain was standing with his back against the door, pale to the lips.

"There is something in that berth!" he cried, in a strange voice, his eyes almost starting from his head. "Hold the door, while I look—it shall not escape us, whatever it is!"

But instead of taking his place, I sprang upon the lower bed, and seized something which lay in the upper berth.

It was something ghostly, horrible beyond words, and it moved in my grip. It was like the body of a man long drowned, and yet it moved, and had the strength of ten men living; but I gripped it with all my might—the slippery, oozy, horrible thing. The dead white eyes seemed to stare at me out of the dusk; the putrid odour of rank sea-water was about it, and its shiny hair hung in foul wet curls over its dead face. I wrestled with the dead thing; it thrust itself upon me and forced me back and nearly broke my arms; it wound its corpse's arms about my neck, the living death, and overpowered me, so that I, at last, cried aloud and fell, and left my hold.

As I fell the thing sprang across me, and seemed to throw itself upon the captain. When I last saw him on his feet his face was white and his lips set. It seemed to me that he struck a violent blow at the dead being, and then he, too, fell forward upon his face, with an inarticulate cry of horror.

The thing paused an instant, seeming to hover over his prostrate body, and I could have screamed again for very fright, but I had no voice left. The thing vanished suddenly, and it seemed to my disturbed senses that it made its exit through the open port, though how that was possible, considering the smallness of the aperture, is more than any one can tell. I lay a long time upon the floor, and the captain lay beside me. At last I partially recovered my senses and moved, and I instantly knew that my arm was broken—the small bone of the left forearm near the wrist.

I got upon my feet somehow, and with my remaining hand I tried to raise the captain. He groaned and moved, and at last came to himself. He was not hurt, but he seemed badly stunned.

Well, do you want to hear any more? There is nothing more. That is the end of my story. The carpenter carried out his scheme of running half a dozen four-inch screws through the door of one hundred and five; and if ever you take a passage in the Kamtschatka, you may ask for a berth in that state-room. You will be told that it is engaged—yes—it is engaged by that dead thing.

I finished the trip in the surgeon's cabin. He doctored my broken arm, and advised me not to "fiddle about with ghosts and things" any more. The captain was very silent, and never sailed again in that ship, though it is still running. And I will not sail in her either. It was a very disagreeable experience, and I was very badly frightened, which is a thing I do not like. That is all. That is how I saw a ghost—if it was a ghost. It was dead, anyhow.

BY THE WATERS OF PARADISE

I

I remember my childhood very distinctly. I do not think that the fact argues a good memory, for I have never been clever at learning words by heart, in prose or rhyme; so that I believe my remembrance of events depends much more upon the events themselves than upon my possessing any special facility for recalling them. Perhaps I am too imaginative, and the earliest impressions I received were of a kind to stimulate the imagination abnormally. A long series of little misfortunes, connected with each other as to suggest a sort of weird fatality, so worked upon my melancholy temperament when I was a boy that, before I was of age, I sincerely believed myself to be under a curse, and not only myself, but my whole family, and every individual who bore my name.

I was born in the old place where my father, and his father, and all his predecessors had been born, beyond the memory of man. It is a very old house, and the greater part of it was originally a castle, strongly fortified, and surrounded by a deep moat supplied with abundant water from the hills by a hidden aqueduct. Many of the fortifications have been destroyed, and the moat has been filled up. The water from the aqueduct supplies great fountains, and runs down into huge oblong basins in the terraced gardens, one below the other, each surrounded by a broad pavement of marble between the water and the flower-beds. The waste surplus finally escapes through an artificial grotto, some thirty yards long, into a stream, flowing down through the park to the meadows beyond, and thence to the distant river. The buildings were extended a little and greatly altered more than two hundred years ago, in the time of Charles II., but since then little has been done to improve them, though they have been kept in fairly good repair, according to our fortunes.

In the gardens there are terraces and huge hedges of box and evergreen, some of which used to be clipped into shapes of animals, in the Italian style. I can remember when I was a lad how I used to try to make out what the trees were cut to represent, and how I used to appeal for explanations to Judith, my Welsh nurse. She dealt in a strange mythology of her own, and peopled the gardens with griffins, dragons, good genii and bad, and filled my mind with them at the same time. My nursery window afforded a view of the great fountains at the head of the upper basin, and on moonlight nights the Welshwoman would hold me up to the glass and bid me look at the mist and spray rising into mysterious shapes, moving mystically in the white light like living things.

"It's the Woman of the Water," she used to say; and sometimes she would threaten that if I did not go to sleep the Woman of the Water would steal up to the high window and carry me away in her wet arms.

The place was gloomy. The broad basins of water and the tall evergreen hedges gave it a funereal look, and the damp-stained marble causeways by the pools might have been made of tombstones.

The gray and weather-beaten walls and towers without, the dark and massively-furnished rooms within, the deep, mysterious recesses and the heavy curtains, all affected my spirits. I was silent and sad from my childhood. There was a great clock tower above, from which the hours rang dismally during the day, and tolled like a knell in the dead of night. There was no light nor life in the house, for my mother was a helpless invalid, and my father had grown melancholy in his long task of caring for her. He was a thin, dark man, with sad eyes; kind, I think, but silent and unhappy. Next to my mother, I believe he loved me better than anything on earth, for he took immense pains and trouble in teaching me, and what he taught me I have never forgotten. Perhaps it was his only amusement, and that may be the reason why I had no nursery governess or teacher of any kind while he lived.

I used to be taken to see my mother every day, and sometimes twice a day, for an hour at a time. Then I sat upon a little stool near her feet, and she would ask me what I had been doing, and what I wanted to do. I daresay she saw already the seeds of a profound melancholy in my nature, for she looked at me always with a sad smile, and kissed me with a sigh when I was taken away.

One night, when I was just six years old, I lay awake in the nursery. The door was not quite shut, and the Welsh nurse was sitting sewing in the next room. Suddenly I heard her groan, and say in a strange voice, "One—two—one—two!" I was frightened, and I jumped up and ran to the door, barefooted as I was.

"What is it, Judith?" I cried, clinging to her skirts. I can remember the look in her strange dark eyes as she answered.

"One—two leaden coffins, fallen from the ceiling!" she crooned, working herself in her chair. "One—two—a light coffin and a heavy coffin, falling to the floor!"

Then she seemed to notice me, and she took me back to bed and sang me to sleep with a queer old Welsh song.

I do not know how it was, but the impression got hold of me that she had meant that my father and mother were going to die very soon. They died in the very room where she had been sitting that night. It was a great room, my day nursery, full of sun when there was any: and when the days were dark it was the most cheerful place in the house. My mother grew rapidly worse, and I was transferred to another part of the building to make place for her. They thought my nursery was gayer for her, I suppose; but she could not live. She was beautiful when she was dead, and I cried bitterly.

"The light one, the light one—the heavy one to come," crooned the Welshwoman. And she was right. My father took the room after my mother was gone, and day by day he grew thinner and paler and sadder.

"The heavy one, the heavy one—all of lead," moaned my nurse, one night in December, standing still, just as she was going to take away the light after putting me to bed. Then she took me up again and wrapped me in a little gown, and led me away to my father's room. She knocked, but no one answered. She opened the door, and we found him in his easy-chair before the fire, very white, quite dead.

So I was alone with the Welshwoman till strange people came, and relations whom I had never seen; and then I heard them saying that I must be taken away to some more cheerful place. They were kind people, and I will not believe that they were kind only because I was to be very rich when I grew to be a man. The world never seemed to be a very bad place to me, nor all the people to be miserable sinners, even when I was most melancholy. I do not remember that any one ever did me any great injustice, nor that I was ever oppressed or ill-treated in any way, even by the boys at school. I was sad, I suppose, because my childhood was so gloomy, and, later, because I was unlucky in everything I undertook, till I finally believed I was pursued by fate, and I used to dream that the old Welsh nurse and the Woman of the Water between them had vowed to pursue me to my end. But my natural disposition should have been cheerful, as I have often thought.

Among lads of my age I was never last, or even among the last, in anything; but I was never first. If I trained for a race, I was sure to sprain my ankle on the day when I was to run. If I pulled an oar with others, my oar was sure to break. If I competed for a prize, some unforeseen accident prevented my winning it at the last moment. Nothing to which I put my hand succeeded, and I got the reputation of being unlucky, until my companions felt it was always safe to bet against me, no matter what the appearances might be. I became discouraged and listless in everything. I gave up the idea of competing for any distinction at the University, comforting myself with the thought that I could not fail in the examination for the ordinary degree. The day before the examination began I fell ill; and when at last I recovered, after a narrow escape from death, I turned my back upon Oxford, and went down alone to visit the old place where I had been born, feeble in health and profoundly disgusted and discouraged. I was twenty-one years of age, master of myself and of my fortune; but so deeply had the long chain of small unlucky circumstances affected me that I thought seriously of shutting myself up from the world to live the life of a hermit, and to die as soon as possible. Death seemed the only cheerful possibility in my existence, and my thoughts soon dwelt upon it altogether.

I had never shown any wish to return to my own home since I had been taken away as a little boy, and no one had ever pressed me to do so. The place had been kept in order after a fashion, and did not seem to have suffered during the fifteen years or more of my absence. Nothing earthly could affect those old grey walls that had fought the elements for so many centuries. The garden was more wild than I remembered it; the marble causeways about the pools looked more yellow and damp than of old, and the whole place at first looked smaller. It was not until I had wandered about the house and grounds for many hours that I realised the huge size of the home where I was to live in solitude. Then I began to delight in it, and my resolution to live alone grew stronger.

The people had turned out to welcome me, of course, and I tried to recognise the changed faces of the old gardener and the old housekeeper, and to call them by name. My old nurse I knew at once. She had grown very grey since she heard the coffins fall in the nursery fifteen years before, but her strange eyes were the same, and the look in them woke all my old memories. She went over the house with me.

"And how is the Woman of the Water?" I asked, trying to laugh a little. "Does she still play in the moonlight?"

"She is hungry," answered the Welshwoman, in a low voice.

"Hungry? Then we will feed her." I laughed. But old Judith turned very pale, and looked at me strangely.

"Feed her? Ay—you will feed her well," she muttered, glancing behind her at the ancient housekeeper, who tottered after us with feeble steps through the halls and passages.

I did not think much of her words. She had always talked oddly, as Welshwomen will, and though I was very melancholy I am sure I was not superstitious, and I was certainly not timid. Only, as in a far-off dream, I seemed to see her standing with the light in her hand and muttering, "The heavy one—all of lead," and then leading a little boy through the long corridors to see his father lying dead in a great easy-chair before a smouldering fire. So we went over the house, and I chose the rooms where I would live; and the servants I had brought with me ordered and arranged everything, and I had no more trouble. I did not care what they did provided I was left in peace, and was not expected to give directions; for I was more listless than ever, owing to the effects of my illness at college.

I dined in solitary state, and the melancholy grandeur of the vast old dining-room pleased me. Then I went to the room I had selected for my study, and sat down in a deep chair, under a bright light, to think, or to let my thoughts meander through labyrinths of their own choosing, utterly indifferent to the course they might take.

The tall windows of the room opened to the level of the ground upon the terrace at the head of the garden. It was in the end of July, and everything was open, for the weather was warm. As I sat alone I heard the unceasing plash of the great fountains, and I fell to thinking of the Woman of the Water. I rose, and went out into the still night, and sat down upon a seat on the terrace, between two gigantic Italian flower-pots. The air was deliciously soft and sweet with the smell of the flowers, and the garden was more congenial to me than the house. Sad people always like running water and the sound of it at night, though I cannot tell why. I sat and listened in the gloom, for it was dark below, and the pale moon had not yet climbed over the hills in front of me, though all the air above was light with her rising beams. Slowly the white halo in the eastern sky ascended in an arch above the wooded crests, making the outlines of the mountains more intensely black by contrast, as though the head of some great white saint were rising from behind a screen in a vast cathedral, throwing misty glories from below. I longed to see the moon herself, and I tried to reckon the seconds before she must appear. Then she sprang up quickly, and in a moment more hung round and perfect in the sky. I gazed at her, and then at the floating spray of the tall fountains, and down at the pools, where the water-lilies were rocking softly in their sleep on the velvet surface of the moon-lit water. Just then a great swan floated out silently into the midst of the basin, and wreathed his long neck, catching the water in his broad bill, and scattering showers of diamonds around him.

Suddenly, as I gazed, something came between me and the light. I looked up instantly. Between me and the round disk of the moon rose a luminous face of a woman, with great strange eyes, and a woman's mouth, full and soft, but not smiling, hooded in black, staring at me as I sat still upon my bench. She was close to me—so close that I could have touched her with my hand. But I was transfixed and helpless. She stood still for a moment, but her expression did not change. Then she passed swiftly away, and my hair stood up on my head, while the cold breeze from her white dress was wafted to my temples as she moved. The moonlight, shining through the tossing spray of the fountain, made traceries of shadow on the gleaming folds of her garments. In an instant she was gone and I was alone.

I was strangely shaken by the vision, and some time passed before I could rise to my feet, for I was still weak from my illness, and the sight I had seen would have startled any one. I did not reason with myself, for I was certain that I had looked on the unearthly, and no argument could have destroyed that belief. At last I got up and stood unsteadily, gazing in the direction in which I thought the face had gone; but there was nothing to be seen—nothing but the broad paths, the tall, dark evergreen hedges, the tossing water of the fountains and the smooth pool below. I fell back upon the seat and recalled the face I had seen. Strange to say, now that the first impression had passed, there was nothing startling in the recollection; on the contrary, I felt that I was fascinated by the face, and would give anything to see it again. I could retrace the beautiful straight features, the long dark eyes, and the wonderful mouth most exactly in my mind, and when I had reconstructed every detail from memory I knew that the whole was beautiful, and that I should love a woman with such a face.

"I wonder whether she is the Woman of the Water!" I said to myself. Then rising once more, I wandered down the garden, descending one short flight of steps after another, from terrace to terrace by the edge of the marble basins, through the shadow and through the moonlight; and I crossed the water by the rustic bridge above the artificial grotto, and climbed slowly up again to the highest terrace by the other side. The air seemed sweeter, and I was very calm, so that I think I smiled to myself as I walked, as though a new happiness had come to me. The woman's face seemed always before me, and the thought of it gave me an unwonted thrill of pleasure, unlike anything I had ever felt before.

I turned, as I reached the house, and looked back upon the scene. It had certainly changed in the short hour since I had come out, and my mood had changed with it. Just like my luck, I thought, to fall in love with a ghost! But in old times I would have sighed, and gone to bed more sad than ever, at such a melancholy conclusion. To-night I felt happy, almost for the first time in my life. The gloomy old study seemed cheerful when I went in. The old pictures on the walls smiled at me, and I sat down in my deep chair with a new and delightful sensation that I was not alone. The idea of having seen a ghost, and of feeling much the better for it, was so absurd that I laughed softly, as I took up one of the books I had brought with me and began to read.

That impression did not wear off. I slept peacefully, and in the morning I threw open my windows to the summer air and looked down at the garden, at the stretches of green and at the coloured flower-beds, at the circling swallows and at the bright water.

"A man might make a paradise of this place," I exclaimed. "A man and a woman together!"

From that day the old castle no longer seemed gloomy, and I think I ceased to be sad; for some time, too, I began to take an interest in the place, and to try and make it more alive. I avoided my old Welsh nurse, lest she should damp my humour with some dismal prophecy, and recall my old self by bringing back memories of my dismal childhood. But what I thought of most was the ghostly figure I had seen in the garden that first night after my arrival. I went out every evening and wandered through the walks and paths; but, try as I might, I did not see my vision again. At last, after many days, the memory grew more faint, and my old moody nature gradually overcame the temporary sense of lightness I had experienced. The summer turned to autumn, and I grew restless. It began to rain. The dampness pervaded the gardens, and the outer halls smelled musty, like tombs; the grey sky oppressed me intolerably. I left the place as it was and went abroad, determined to try anything which might possibly make a second break in the monotonous melancholy from which I suffered.

II

Most people would be struck by the utter insignificance of the small events which, after the death of my parents, influenced my life and made me unhappy. The gruesome forebodings of a Welsh nurse, which chanced to be realised by an odd coincidence of events, should not seem enough to change the nature of a child, and to direct the bent of his character in after years. The little disappointments of schoolboy life, and the somewhat less childish ones of an uneventful and undistinguished academic career, should not have sufficed to turn me out at one-and-twenty years of age a melancholic, listless idler. Some weakness of my own character may have contributed to the result, but in a greater degree it was due to my having a reputation for bad luck. However, I will not try to analyse the causes of my state, for I should satisfy nobody, least of all myself. Still less will I attempt to explain why I felt a temporary revival of my spirits after my adventure in the garden. It is certain that I was in love with the face I had seen, and that I longed to see it again; that I gave up all hope of a second visitation, grew more sad than ever, packed up my traps, and finally went abroad. But in my dreams I went back to my home, and it always appeared to me sunny and bright, as it had looked on that summer's morning after I had seen the woman by the fountain.

I went to Paris. I went further, and wandered about Germany. I tried to amuse myself, and I failed miserably. With the aimless whims of an idle and useless man, come all sorts of suggestions for good resolutions. One day I made up my mind that I would go and bury myself in a German university for a time, and live simply like a poor student. I started with the intention of going to Leipsic, determined to stay there until some event should direct my life or change my humour, or make an end of me altogether. The express train stopped at some station of which I did not know the name. It was dusk on a winter's afternoon, and I peered through the thick glass from my seat. Suddenly another train came gliding in from the opposite direction, and stopped alongside of ours. I looked at the carriage which chanced to be abreast of mine, and idly read the black letters painted on a white board swinging from the brass handrail: BERLIN—COLOGNE—PARIS. Then I looked up at the window above. I started violently, and the cold perspiration broke out upon my forehead. In the dim light, not six feet from where I sat, I saw the face of a woman, the face I loved, the straight, fine features, the strange eyes, the wonderful mouth, the pale skin. Her head-dress was a dark veil, which seemed to be tied about her head and passed over the shoulders under her chin. As I threw down the window and knelt on the cushioned seat, leaning far out to get a better view, a long whistle screamed through the station, followed by a quick series of dull, clanking sounds; then there was a slight jerk, and my train moved on. Luckily the window was narrow, being the one over the seat, beside the door, or I believe I would have jumped out of it then and there. In an instant the speed increased, and I was being carried swiftly away in the opposite direction from the thing I loved.

For a quarter of an hour I lay back in my place, stunned by the suddenness of the apparition. At last one of the two other passengers, a large and gorgeous captain of the White Konigsberg Cuirassiers, civilly but firmly suggested that I might shut my window, as the evening was cold. I did so, with an apology, and relapsed into silence. The train ran swiftly on, for a long time, and it was already beginning to slacken speed before entering another station, when I roused myself and made a sudden resolution. As the carriage stopped before the brilliantly lighted platform, I seized my belongings, saluted my fellow-passengers, and got out, determined to take the first express back to Paris.

This time the circumstances of the vision had been so natural that it did not strike me that there was anything unreal about the face, or about the woman to whom it belonged. I did not try to explain to myself how the face, and the woman, could be travelling by a fast train from Berlin to Paris on a winter's afternoon, when both were in my mind indelibly associated with the moonlight and the fountains in my own English home. I certainly would not have admitted that I had been mistaken in the dusk, attributing to what I had seen a resemblance to my former vision which did not really exist. There was not the slightest doubt in my mind, and I was positively sure that I had again seen the face I loved. I did not hesitate, and in a few hours I was on my way back to Paris. I could not help reflecting on my ill luck. Wandering as I had been for many months, it might as easily have chanced that I should be travelling in the same train with that woman, instead of going the other way. But my luck was destined to turn for a time.

I searched Paris for several days. I dined at the principal hotels; I went to the theatres; I rode in the Bois de Boulogne in the morning, and picked up an acquaintance, whom I forced to drive with me in the afternoon. I went to mass at the Madeleine, and I attended the services at the English Church. I hung about the Louvre and Notre Dame. I went to Versailles. I spent hours in parading the Rue de Rivoli, in the neighbourhood of Meurice's corner, where foreigners pass and repass from morning till night. At last I received an invitation to a reception at the English Embassy. I went, and I found what I had sought so long.

There she was, sitting by an old lady in grey satin and diamonds, who had a wrinkled but kindly face and keen grey eyes that seemed to take in everything they saw, with very little inclination to give much in return. But I did not notice the chaperon. I saw only the face that had haunted me for months, and in the excitement of the moment I walked quickly towards the pair, forgetting such a trifle as the necessity for an introduction.

She was far more beautiful than I had thought, but I never doubted that it was she herself and no other. Vision or no vision before, this was the reality, and I knew it. Twice her hair had been covered, now at last I saw it, and the added beauty of its magnificence glorified the whole woman. It was rich hair, fine and abundant, golden, with deep ruddy tints in it like red bronze spun fine. There was no ornament in it, not a rose, not a thread of gold, and I felt that it needed nothing to enhance its splendour; nothing but her pale face, her dark strange eyes, and her heavy eyebrows. I could see that she was slender too, but strong withal, as she sat there quietly gazing at the moving scene in the midst of the brilliant lights and the hum of perpetual conversation.

I recollected the detail of introduction in time, and turned aside to look for my host. I found him at last. I begged him to present me to the two ladies, pointing them out to him at the same time.

"Yes—uh—by all means—uh—" replied his Excellency with a pleasant smile. He evidently had no idea of my name, which was not to be wondered at.

"I am Lord Cairngorm," I observed.

"Oh—by all means," answered the Ambassador with the same hospitable smile. "Yes—uh—the fact is, I must try and find out who they are; such lots of people, you know."

"Oh, if you will present me, I will try and find out for you," said I, laughing.

"Ah, yes—so kind of you—come along," said my host. We threaded the crowd, and in a few minutes we stood before the two ladies.

"'Lowmintrduce L'd Cairngorm," he said; then, adding quickly to me, "Come and dine to-morrow, won't you?" he glided away with his pleasant smile and disappeared in the crowd.

I sat down beside the beautiful girl, conscious that the eyes of the duenna were upon me.

"I think we have been very near meeting before," I remarked, by way of opening the conversation.

My companion turned her eyes full upon me with an air of inquiry. She evidently did not recall my face, if she had ever seen me.

"Really—I cannot remember," she observed, in a low and musical voice. "When?"

"In the first place, you came down from Berlin by the express, ten days ago. I was going the other way, and our carriages stopped opposite each other. I saw you at the window."

"Yes—we came that way, but I do not remember—" She hesitated.

"Secondly," I continued, "I was sitting alone in my garden last summer—near the end of July—do you remember? You must have wandered in there through the park; you came up to the house and looked at me—"

"Was that you?" she asked, in evident surprise. Then she broke into a laugh. "I told everybody I had seen a ghost; there had never been any Cairngorms in the place since the memory of man. We left the next day, and never heard that you had come there; indeed, I did not know the castle belonged to you."

"Where were you staying?" I asked.

"Where? Why, with my aunt, where I always stay. She is your neighbour, since it is you."

"I—beg your pardon—but then—is your aunt Lady Bluebell? I did not quite catch—"

"Don't be afraid. She is amazingly deaf. Yes. She is the relict of my beloved uncle, the sixteenth or seventeenth Baron Bluebell—I forget exactly how many of them there have been. And I—do you know who I am?" She laughed, well knowing that I did not.

"No," I answered frankly. "I have not the least idea. I asked to be introduced because I recognised you. Perhaps—perhaps you are a Miss Bluebell?"

"Considering that you are a neighbour, I will tell you who I am," she answered. "No; I am of the tribe of Bluebells, but my name is Lammas, and I have been given to understand that I was christened Margaret. Being a floral family, they call me Daisy. A dreadful American man once told me that my aunt was a Bluebell and that I was a Harebell—with two l's and an e—because my hair is so thick. I warn you, so that you may avoid making such a bad pun."

"Do I look like a man who makes puns?" I asked, being very conscious of my melancholy face and sad looks.

Miss Lammas eyed me critically.

"No; you have a mournful temperament. I think I can trust you," she answered. "Do you think you could communicate to my aunt the fact that you are a Cairngorm and a neighbour? I am sure she would like to know."

I leaned towards the old lady, inflating my lungs for a yell. But Miss Lammas stopped me.

"That is not of the slightest use," she remarked. "You can write it on a bit of paper. She is utterly deaf."

"I have a pencil," I answered; "but I have no paper. Would my cuff do, do you think?"

"Oh, yes!" replied Miss Lammas, with alacrity; "men often do that."

I wrote on my cuff: "Miss Lammas wishes me to explain that I am your neighbour, Cairngorm." Then I held out my arm before the old lady's nose. She seemed perfectly accustomed to the proceeding, put up her glasses, read the words, smiled, nodded, and addressed me in the unearthly voice peculiar to people who hear nothing.

"I knew your grandfather very well," she said. Then she smiled and nodded to me again, and to her niece, and relapsed into silence.

"It is all right," remarked Miss Lammas. "Aunt Bluebell knows she is deaf, and does not say much, like the parrot. You see, she knew your grandfather. How odd, that we should be neighbours! Why have we never met before?"

"If you had told me you knew my grandfather when you appeared in the garden, I should not have been in the least surprised," I answered rather irrelevantly. "I really thought you were the ghost of the old fountain. How in the world did you come there at that hour?"

"We were a large party and we went out for a walk. Then we thought we should like to see what your park was like in the moonlight, and so we trespassed. I got separated from the rest, and came upon you by accident, just as I was admiring the extremely ghostly look of your house, and wondering whether anybody would ever come and live there again. It looks like the castle of Macbeth, or a scene from the opera. Do you know anybody here?"

"Hardly a soul! Do you?"

"No. Aunt Bluebell said it was our duty to come. It is easy for her to go out; she does not bear the burden of the conversation."

"I am sorry you find it a burden," said I. "Shall I go away?"

Miss Lammas looked at me with a sudden gravity in her beautiful eyes, and there was a sort of hesitation about the lines of her full, soft mouth.

"No," she said at last, quite simply, "don't go away. We may like each other, if you stay a little longer—and we ought to, because we are neighbours in the country."

I suppose I ought to have thought Miss Lammas a very odd girl. There is, indeed, a sort of freemasonry between people who discover that they live near each other, and that they ought to have known each other before. But there was a sort of unexpected frankness and simplicity in the girl's amusing manner which would have struck any one else as being singular, to say the least of it. To me, however, it all seemed natural enough. I had dreamed of her face too long not to be utterly happy when I met her at last, and could talk to her as much as I pleased. To me, the man of ill luck in everything, the whole meeting seemed too good to be true. I felt again that strange sensation of lightness which I had experienced after I had seen her face in the garden. The great rooms seemed brighter, life seemed worth living; my sluggish, melancholy blood ran faster, and filled me with a new sense of strength. I said to myself that without this woman I was but an imperfect being, but that with her I could accomplish everything to which I should set my hand. Like the great Doctor, when he thought he had cheated Mephistopheles at last, I could have cried aloud to the fleeting moment, Verweile doch, du bist so schön!

"Are you always gay?" I asked, suddenly. "How happy you must be!"

"The days would sometimes seem very long if I were gloomy," she answered, thoughtfully. "Yes, I think I find life very pleasant, and I tell it so."

"How can you 'tell life' anything?" I inquired. "If I could catch my life and talk to it, I would abuse it prodigiously, I assure you."

"I daresay. You have a melancholy temper. You ought to live out of doors, dig potatoes, make hay, shoot, hunt, tumble into ditches, and come home muddy and hungry for dinner. It would be much better for you than moping in your rook tower, and hating everything."

"It is rather lonely down there," I murmured, apologetically, feeling that Miss Lammas was quite right.

"Then marry, and quarrel with your wife," she laughed. "Anything is better than being alone."

"I am a very peaceable person. I never quarrel with anybody. You can try it. You will find it quite impossible."

"Will you let me try?" she asked, still smiling.

"By all means—especially if it is to be only a preliminary canter," I answered, rashly.

"What do you mean?" she inquired, turning quickly upon me.

"Oh—nothing. You might try my paces with a view to quarrelling in the future. I cannot imagine how you are going to do it. You will have to resort to immediate and direct abuse."

"No. I will only say that if you do not like your life, it is your own fault. How can a man of your age talk of being melancholy, or of the hollowness of existence? Are you consumptive? Are you subject to hereditary insanity? Are you deaf, like Aunt Bluebell? Are you poor, like—lots of people? Have you been crossed in love? Have you lost the world for a woman, or any particular woman for the sake of the world? Are you feeble-minded, a cripple, an outcast? Are you—repulsively ugly?" She laughed again. "Is there any reason in the world why you should not enjoy all you have got in life?"

"No. There is no reason whatever, except that I am dreadfully unlucky, especially in small things."

"Then try big things, just for a change," suggested Miss Lammas. "Try and get married, for instance, and see how it turns out."

"If it turned out badly it would be rather serious."

"Not half so serious as it is to abuse everything unreasonably. If abuse is your particular talent, abuse something that ought to be abused. Abuse the Conservatives—or the Liberals—it does not matter which, since they are always abusing each other. Make yourself felt by other people. You will like it, if they don't. It will make a man of you. Fill your mouth with pebbles, and howl at the sea, if you cannot do anything else. It did Demosthenes no end of good you know. You will have the satisfaction of imitating a great man."

"Really, Miss Lammas, I think the list of innocent exercises you propose—"

"Very well—if you don't care for that sort of thing, care for some other sort of thing. Care for something, or hate something. Don't be idle. Life is short, and though art may be long, plenty of noise answers nearly as well."

"I do care for something—I mean, somebody," I said.

"A woman? Then marry her. Don't hesitate."

"I do not know whether she would marry me," I replied. "I have never asked her."

"Then ask her at once," answered Miss Lammas. "I shall die happy if I feel I have persuaded a melancholy fellow-creature to rouse himself to action. Ask her, by all means, and see what she says. If she does not accept you at once, she may take you the next time. Meanwhile, you will have entered for the race. If you lose, there are the 'All-aged Trial Stakes,' and the 'Consolation Race.'"

"And plenty of selling races into the bargain. Shall I take you at your word, Miss Lammas?"

"I hope you will," she answered.

"Since you yourself advise me, I will. Miss Lammas, will you do me the honour to marry me?"

For the first time in my life the blood rushed to my head and my sight swam. I cannot tell why I said it. It would be useless to try to explain the extraordinary fascination the girl exercised over me, nor the still more extraordinary feeling of intimacy with her which had grown in me during that half-hour. Lonely, sad, unlucky as I had been all my life, I was certainly not timid, nor even shy. But to propose to marry a woman after half an hour's acquaintance was a piece of madness of which I never believed myself capable, and of which I should never be capable again, could I be placed in the same situation. It was as though my whole being had been changed in a moment by magic—by the white magic of her nature brought into contact with mine. The blood sank back to my heart, and a moment later I found myself staring at her with anxious eyes. To my amazement she was as calm as ever, but her beautiful mouth smiled, and there was a mischievous light in her dark-brown eyes.

"Fairly caught," she answered. "For an individual who pretends to be listless and sad you are not lacking in humour. I had really not the least idea what you were going to say. Wouldn't it be singularly awkward for you if I had said 'Yes'? I never saw anybody begin to practise so sharply what was preached to him—with so very little loss of time!"

"You probably never met a man who had dreamed of you for seven months before being introduced."

"No, I never did," she answered, gaily. "It smacks of the romantic. Perhaps you are a romantic character, after all. I should think you were if I believed you. Very well; you have taken my advice, entered for a Stranger's Race and lost it. Try the All-aged Trial Stakes. You have another cuff, and a pencil. Propose to Aunt Bluebell; she would dance with astonishment, and she might recover her hearing."

III

That was how I first asked Margaret Lammas to be my wife, and I will agree with any one who says I behaved very foolishly. But I have not repented of it, and I never shall. I have long ago understood that I was out of my mind that evening, but I think my temporary insanity on that occasion has had the effect of making me a saner man ever since. Her manner turned my head, for it was so different from what I had expected. To hear this lovely creature, who, in my imagination, was a heroine of romance, if not of tragedy, talking familiarly and laughing readily was more than my equanimity could bear, and I lost my head as well as my heart. But when I went back to England in the spring, I went to make certain arrangements at the Castle—certain changes and improvements which would be absolutely necessary. I had won the race for which I had entered myself so rashly, and we were to be married in June.

Whether the change was due to the orders I had left with the gardener and the rest of the servants, or to my own state of mind, I cannot tell. At all events, the old place did not look the same to me when I opened my window on the morning after my arrival. There were the grey walls below me, and the grey turrets flanking the huge building; there were the fountains, the marble causeways, the smooth basins, the tall box hedges, the water-lilies and the swans, just as of old. But there was something else there, too—something in the air, in the water, and in the greenness that I did not recognise—a light over everything by which everything was transfigured. The clock in the tower struck seven, and the strokes of the ancient bell sounded like a wedding chime. The air sang with the thrilling treble of the songbirds, with the silvery music of the plashing water and the softer harmony of the leaves stirred by the fresh morning wind. There was a smell of new-mown hay from the distant meadows, and of blooming roses from the beds below, wafted up together to my window. I stood in the pure sunshine and drank the air and all the sounds and the odours that were in it; and I looked down at my garden and said: "It is Paradise, after all." I think the men of old were right when they called heaven a garden, and Eden, a garden inhabited by one man and one woman, the Earthly Paradise.

I turned away, wondering what had become of the gloomy memories I had always associated with my home. I tried to recall the impression of my nurse's horrible prophecy before the death of my parents—an impression which hitherto had been vivid enough. I tried to remember my old self, my dejection, my listlessness, my bad luck, and my petty disappointments. I endeavoured to force myself to think as I used to think, if only to satisfy myself that I had not lost my individuality. But I succeeded in none of these efforts. I was a different man, a changed being, incapable of sorrow, of ill luck, or of sadness. My life had been a dream, not evil, but infinitely gloomy and hopeless. It was now a reality, full of hope, gladness, and all manner of good. My home had been like a tomb; to-day it was paradise. My heart had been as though it had not existed; to-day it beat with strength and youth, and the certainty of realised happiness. I revelled in the beauty of the world, and called loveliness out of the future to enjoy it before time should bring it to me, as a traveller in the plains looks up to the mountains, and already tastes the cool air through the dust of the road.

Here, I thought, we will live and live for years. There we will sit by the fountain towards evening and in the deep moonlight. Down those paths we will wander together. On those benches we will rest and talk. Among those eastern hills we will ride through the soft twilight, and in the old house we will tell tales on winter nights, when the logs burn high, and the holly berries are red, and the old clock tolls out the dying year. On these old steps, in these dark passages and stately rooms, there will one day be the sound of little pattering feet, and laughing child-voices will ring up to the vaults of the ancient hall. Those tiny footsteps shall not be slow and sad as mine were, nor shall the childish words be spoken in an awed whisper. No gloomy Welshwoman shall people the dusky corners with weird horrors, nor utter horrid prophecies of death and ghastly things. All shall be young, and fresh, and joyful, and happy, and we will turn the old luck again, and forget that there was ever any sadness.

So I thought, as I looked out of my window that morning and for many mornings after that, and every day it all seemed more real than ever before, and much nearer. But the old nurse looked at me askance, and muttered odd sayings about the Woman of the Water. I cared little what she said, for I was far too happy.

At last the time came near for the wedding. Lady Bluebell and all the tribe of Bluebells, as Margaret called them, were at Bluebell Grange, for we had determined to be married in the country, and to come straight to the Castle afterwards. We cared little for travelling, and not at all for a crowded ceremony at St. George's in Hanover Square, with all the tiresome formalities afterwards. I used to ride over to the Grange every day, and very often Margaret would come with her aunt and some of her cousins to the Castle. I was suspicious of my own taste, and was only too glad to let her have her way about the alterations and improvements in our home.

We were to be married on the thirtieth of July, and on the evening of the twenty-eighth Margaret drove over with some of the Bluebell party. In the long summer twilight we all went out into the garden. Naturally enough, Margaret and I were left to ourselves, and we wandered down by the marble basins.

"It is an odd coincidence," I said; "it was on this very night last year that I first saw you."

"Considering that it is the month of July," answered Margaret with a laugh, "and that we have been here almost every day, I don't think the coincidence is so extraordinary, after all."

"No, dear," said I, "I suppose not. I don't know why it struck me. We shall very likely be here a year from to-day, and a year from that. The odd thing, when I think of it, is that you should be here at all. But my luck has turned. I ought not to think anything odd that happens now that I have you. It is all sure to be good."

"A slight change in your ideas since that remarkable performance of yours in Paris," said Margaret. "Do you know, I thought you were the most extraordinary man I had ever met."

"I thought you were the most charming woman I had ever seen. I naturally did not want to lose any time in frivolities. I took you at your word, I followed your advice, I asked you to marry me, and this is the delightful result—what's the matter?"

Margaret had started suddenly, and her hand tightened on my arm. An old woman was coming up the path, and was close to us before we saw her, for the moon had risen, and was shining full in our faces. The woman turned out to be my old nurse.

"It's only old Judith, dear—don't be frightened," I said. Then I spoke to the Welshwoman: "What are you about, Judith? Have you been feeding the Woman of the Water?"

"Ay—when the clock strikes, Willie—my lord, I mean," muttered the old creature, drawing aside to let us pass, and fixing her strange eyes on Margaret's face.

"What does she mean?" asked Margaret, when we had gone by.

"Nothing, darling. The old thing is mildly crazy, but she is a good soul."

We went on in silence for a few moments, and came to the rustic bridge just above the artificial grotto through which the water ran out into the park, dark and swift in its narrow channel. We stopped, and leaned on the wooden rail. The moon was now behind us, and shone full upon the long vista of basins and on the huge walls and towers of the Castle above.

"How proud you ought to be of such a grand old place!" said Margaret, softly.

"It is yours now, darling," I answered. "You have as good a right to love it as I—but I only love it because you are to live in it, dear."

Her hand stole out and lay on mine, and we were both silent. Just then the clock began to strike far off in the tower. I counted—eight—nine—ten—eleven—I looked at my watch—twelve—thirteen—I laughed. The bell went on striking.

"The old clock has gone crazy, like Judith," I exclaimed. Still it went on, note after note ringing out monotonously through the still air. We leaned over the rail, instinctively looking in the direction whence the sound came. On and on it went. I counted nearly a hundred, out of sheer curiosity, for I understood that something had broken, and that the thing was running itself down.

Suddenly there was a crack as of breaking wood, a cry and a heavy splash, and I was alone, clinging to the broken end of the rail of the rustic bridge.

I do not think I hesitated while my pulse beat twice. I sprang clear of the bridge into the black rushing water, dived to the bottom, came up again with empty hands, turned and swam downwards through the grotto in the thick darkness, plunging and diving at every stroke, striking my head and hands against jagged stones and sharp corners, clutching at last something in my fingers, and dragging it up with all my might. I spoke, I cried aloud, but there was no answer. I was alone in the pitchy blackness with my burden, and the house was five hundred yards away. Struggling still, I felt the ground beneath my feet, I saw a ray of moonlight—the grotto widened, and the deep water became a broad and shallow brook as I stumbled over the stones and at last laid Margaret's body on the bank in the park beyond.

"Ay, Willie, as the clock struck!" said the voice of Judith, the Welsh nurse, as she bent down and looked at the white face. The old woman must have turned back and followed us, seen the accident, and slipped out by the lower gate of the garden. "Ay," she groaned, "you have fed the Woman of the Water this night, Willie, while the clock was striking."

I scarcely heard her as I knelt beside the lifeless body of the woman I loved, chafing the wet white temples, and gazing wildly into the wide-staring eyes. I remember only the first returning look of consciousness, the first heaving breath, the first movement of those dear hands stretching out towards me.

That is not much of a story, you say. It is the story of my life. That is all. It does not pretend to be anything else. Old Judith says my luck turned on that summer's night, when I was struggling in the water to save all that was worth living for. A month later there was a stone bridge above the grotto, and Margaret and I stood on it and looked up at the moonlit Castle, as we had done once before, and as we have done many times since. For all those things happened ten years ago last summer, and this is the tenth Christmas Eve we have spent together by the roaring logs in the old hall, talking of old times; and every year there are more old times to talk of. There are curly-headed boys, too, with red-gold hair and dark-brown eyes like their mother's, and a little Margaret, with solemn black eyes like mine. Why could not she look like her mother, too, as well as the rest of them?

The world is very bright at this glorious Christmas time, and perhaps there is little use in calling up the sadness of long ago, unless it be to make the jolly firelight seem more cheerful, the good wife's face look gladder, and to give the children's laughter a merrier ring, by contrast with all that is gone. Perhaps, too, some sad-faced, listless, melancholy youth, who feels that the world is very hollow, and that life is like a perpetual funeral service, just as I used to feel myself, may take courage from my example, and having found the woman of his heart, ask her to marry him after half an hour's acquaintance. But, on the whole, I would not advise any man to marry, for the simple reason that no man will ever find a wife like mine, and being obliged to go further, he will necessarily fare worse. My wife has done miracles, but I will not assert that any other woman is able to follow her example.

Margaret always said that the old place was beautiful, and that I ought to be proud of it. I daresay she is right. She has even more imagination than I. But I have a good answer and a plain one, which is this—that all the beauty of the Castle comes from her. She has breathed upon it all, as the children blow upon the cold glass window-panes in winter; and as their warm breath crystallises into landscapes from fairyland, full of exquisite shapes and traceries upon the blank surface, so her spirit has transformed every grey stone of the old towers, every ancient tree and hedge in the gardens, every thought in my once melancholy self. All that was old is young, and all that was sad is glad, and I am the gladdest of all. Whatever heaven may be, there is no earthly paradise without woman, nor is there anywhere a place so desolate, so dreary, so unutterably miserable that a woman cannot make it seem heaven to the man she loves and who loves her.

I hear certain cynics laugh, and cry that all that has been said before. Do not laugh, my good cynic. You are too small a man to laugh at such a great thing as love. Prayers have been said before now by many, and perhaps you say yours, too. I do not think they lose anything by being repeated, nor you by repeating them. You say that the world is bitter, and full of the Waters of Bitterness. Love, and so live that you may be loved—the world will turn sweet for you, and you shall rest like me by the Waters of Paradise.

F. Marion Crawford – A Short Biography

Francis Marion Crawford was born in Bagni di Lucca, Italy on 2nd August, 1854, the only son of the American sculptor Thomas Crawford and Louisa Cutler Ward. His aunt was Julia Ward Howe, the American poet, most famous for the words to 'The Battle Hymn of the Republic'.

After his father's death in 1857, his mother remarried to Luther Terry, with whom she had Crawford's half-sister, Margaret Ward Terry.

Crawford's education began at St Paul's School, Concord, New Hampshire and then went on to Cambridge University, the University of Heidelberg and finally the University of Rome.

In 1879, Crawford went to India to study the ancient language of Sanskrit and to edit Allahabad, The Indian Herald.

Returning to America in February 1881, he enrolled at Harvard University for a year to continue his studies in Sanskrit. Crawford had no real career path at this time although for two years he contributed to various periodicals, mainly The Critic.

Early in 1882, Crawford established a close, lifelong friendship with Isabella Stewart Gardner, a noted and eccentric heiress from Boston who over the years built up a large and eclectic collection of art.

Crawford lived most of his time in Boston with his Aunt Julia and Uncle Sam. The family were concerned by his lack of ambition, prospects in general, and his financial ones in particular.

His mother had hoped he might train in Boston for a career as an operatic baritone based on his private renditions of Schubert lieder. With that in mind it was, in January 1882, that George Henschel, the conductor of the Boston Symphony Orchestra, was called in to assess young Crawford's talents. Henschel was direct and to the point. Crawford would 'never be able to sing in perfect tune'. His Uncle Sam, knowing that Crawford was keen on literary pursuits, proposed that his years in India might be good source material to write about. Crawford agreed. He set to work. Uncle Sam also set about developing contacts with a number of New York publishers.

Events moved very quickly. By December of that year Crawford had completed his first novel, 'Mr Isaacs', based on modern Anglo-Indian life flavoured with a touch of Oriental mystery. It was an immediate success. Crawford set about writing a second novel and the result was 'Dr Claudius' in 1883.

In October 1884 he married Elizabeth Berdan, the daughter of the Civil War Union General Hiram Berdan. The marriage would produce two sons; Harold and Bertram, and two daughters; Eleanor and Clara.

Crawford, buoyed by his excellent start, now decided to return to Italy and to live there permanently.
The couple initially went to Sorrento and lived at the historic Hotel Cocumella during 1885 before moving permanently to Sant' Agnello, where the purchase of the Villa Renzi would now be rededicated as Villa Crawford.

As a writer Crawford had more than his fair share of detractors but, perhaps due to the physical distance between author and these detractors, they did not distract from his prolific output.

Each year seemed to bring a new F. Marion Crawford novel. His popularity was evident although some works, such as 1896's offering 'Adam Johnstone's Son', was described by his left-wing English contemporary, George Gissing, as "rubbish". Over half of his novels are set in Italy. He also wrote three long historical studies of Italy and was nearing completion on a history of Rome in the Middle Ages when he died.

His 'Saracinesca' series are considered his best works. The third in the series, 'Don Orsino' (1892) was told against the background of a real estate bubble and is especially effective. The volume immediately after was 'Corleone' (1897), and the first major treatment of the Mafia in literature.

Crawford himself was fondest of 'Khaled: A Tale of Arabia' (1891), a story of a genie who becomes human. 'A Cigarette-Maker's Romance' (1890) was dramatized, and had considerable popularity on the stage as well as in its novel form.

Towards the end of the 1890's Crawford ventured down another path with his writing. He began his historical works. 'Ave Roma Immortalis' was published in 1898, followed by 'Rulers of the South' (1900), and 'Gleanings from Venetian History' (1905). Most were re-titled with longer more explanatory titles for the American market. Within them all his careful and precise knowledge of the local Italian history together with his literary talents combined to great effect.

Whilst on an American Lecture tour in the winter of 1897-1898 Crawford was researching and gathering technical information for his historical work 'Marietta' (published 1901), that describes glass-making in late medieval Venice. Whilst visiting a glass-smelting plant in Colorado he suffered a severe lung injury when he inhaled toxic gasses. This would eventually contribute to his death a decade or so later.

Crawford's commercial popularity and appeal at the time was such that in 1901, the American Macmillan firm began a deluxe uniform edition of his novels as his works came up for re-printing. In 1904 the P. F. Collier Company in New York was authorized to publish a 25-volume edition (which was later expanded to 32 volumes).

In 1902 he wrote a stage play 'Francesca da Rimini', that was produced in Paris by his friend and legendary actress Sarah Bernhardt.

Towards the end of his life Hollywood had begun to realise that his works were a valuable source of stories and ideas and several were turned into movies and continued to be so for decades after his death.

Crawford also had a gift for pulling off excellent short stories. Several, such as 'The Upper Berth' (1886), 'For the Blood Is the Life' (1905, a vampiress tale), 'The Dead Smile' (1899), and 'The Screaming Skull' (1908), are among the most anthologized classics of the horror genre. After his death several collected volumes were published from various sources.

After most of his fictional works had been published, most had the view that he was a gifted narrator; and his books of fiction, were full of historic vitality and energy as well as dramatic characterization. He was widely popular among readers to whom literature was more for escapism than a confrontation with reality or pages of subjective analysis. In 'The Novel: What It Is' (1893), Crawford was both resolute and disarming in defending his literary approach, self-conceived as a combination of romanticism and realism, defining the art form in terms of its marketplace and audience. The novel, he wrote, is "a marketable commodity" and "intellectual artistic luxury" that "must amuse, indeed, but should amuse reasonably, from an intellectual point of view .... Its intention is to amuse and please, and certainly not to teach and preach; but in order to amuse well it must be a finely-balanced creation ...."

Francis Marion Crawford died at Sorrento on Good Friday 1909 at Villa Crawford of a heart attack.

F. Marion Crawford – A Concise Bibliography

Novels

Mr. Isaacs: A Tale of Modern India (1882)
Dr. Claudius (1883)
To Leeward (1884)
A Roman Singer (1884)
An American Politician (1884)
Zoroaster (1885)
A Tale of a Lonely Parish (1886)
Saracinesca (1887)
Marzio's Crucifix (1887)
Paul Patoff (1887)
With the Immortals (1888)
Greifenstein (1889)
Sant' Ilario (1889); sequel to Saracinesca
A Cigarette-Maker's Romance (1890)

Khaled: A Tale of Arabia (1891)
The Witch of Prague (1891)
The Three Fates (1892)
Don Orsino (1892); sequel to Sant' Ilario
The Children of the King (1893)
Pietro Ghisleri (1893)
Marion Darche (1893)
Katharine Lauderdale (1894)
The Upper Berth (1894); with "By the Waters of Paradise"
Love in Idleness (1894)
The Ralstons (1894); sequel to Katharine Lauderdale
Casa Braccio (1895); related to Katharine Lauderdale and The Ralstons.
Adam Johnstone's Son (1896)
Taquisara (1896)
A Rose of Yesterday (1897)
Corleone (1897)
Via Crucis (1899)
In the Palace of the King (1900)
Marietta (1901)
Cecilia (1902)
Man Overboard! (1903)
The Heart of Rome (1903)
Whosoever Shall Offend (1904)
Soprano (1905); U.S. title: Fair Margaret.
A Lady of Rome (1906)
Arethusa (1907)
The Little City of Hope (1907)
The Primadonna (1908); sequel to Soprano/Fair Margaret
The Diva's Ruby (1908); sequel to The Primadonna
The White Sister (1909)
Stradella (1909)
The Undesirable Governess (1910)
Wandering Ghosts; British title: Uncanny Tales.

Non-fiction

Our Silver (1881)
The Novel: What It Is (1893)
Constantinople (1895)
Bar Harbor (1896)
Ave Roma Immortalis (1898)
Rulers of the South (1900; 1905 in the U.S. as Southern Italy and Sicily and The Rulers of the South)
Gleanings from Venetian History (1905; in the U.S. as Salvae Venetia and in 1909 as Venice; the People and the Place)

Drama

In the Palace of the King (1900) with Lorrimer Stoddard.
Francesca da Rimini (1902) The piece was adapted into an opera by Franco Leoni in 1904.

Evelyn Hastings (1902) Unpublished typescript discovered in 2008.
The White Sister (1909) with Walter C. Hackett.

Filmography

A Cigarette-Maker's Romance, directed by Frank Wilson (UK, 1913, based on the novella)
The White Sister, directed by Fred E. Wright [it] (1915, based on the novel)
In the Palace of the King [it], directed by Fred E. Wright [it] (1915, based on the novel)
Whosoever Shall Offend, directed by Arrigo Bocchi (UK, 1919, based on the novel)
Il cuore di Roma, directed by Edoardo Bencivenga (Italy, 1919, based on the novel)
A Cigarette-Maker's Romance, directed by Tom Watts (UK, 1920, based on the novella)
Saracinesca [it], directed by Gaston Ravel (Italy, 1921, based on the novel)
Sant' Ilario [it], directed by Henry Kolker (Italy, 1923, based on the novel)
The White Sister, directed by Henry King (1923, based on the novel)
In the Palace of the King, directed by Emmett J. Flynn (1923, based on the novel)
Son of India, directed by Jacques Feyder (1931, based on the novel Mr. Isaacs)
The White Sister, directed by Victor Fleming (1933, based on the novel)
The Screaming Skull, directed by Alex Nicol (1958, named after the short story)
The White Sister, directed by Tito Davison (Mexico, 1960, based on the novel)